THE STORIES OF EVERGREEN

BOOK II
PAWNS OF THE IN BETWEEN

I0629740

R. S. HAMILTON

Cover design by RebecaCovers
Second edition January 2026
Paperback ISBN: 979-8-9852548-3-9

VENTURE
Creations LLC

For Stacy Colman,
The one who helped me mold these characters and bring them to life.
I wish you could have stuck around to help me finish this story.
We all miss you!

I'll see you in Evergreen...

Part I: Evergreen

"Donte."

The dragon opened his eyes to a blurry world.

"Donte," the woman's voice was slightly louder this time.

He knew who it was before he opened his eyes. It was Tessa; her hair was pulled back in its usual braid.

"Donte, they need you."

When he raised his head, their eyes met. He sucked in a breath and sighed. He'd been in the same spot for weeks, the same spot since the funeral pyre for Celeste. His only food during that time consisted of the food that Anastasia brought him. She showed up late in the morning, day after day, with a burlap sack partially full of apples. She usually fed him half of what was in the sack. Sometimes she showed up with eggs and snuck him a few.

"Don't tell Momma," she would say as Donte let the eggs roll down the back of his tongue and slip down his throat.

Other than the feedings, he had barely moved.

"They need you at the cabin," Tessa said as she rubbed his nose. "You should leave tonight. Dorn and Raistlin need you. Dorn left and followed the others to the cabin."

Donte perked his head up a little more after hearing Dorn's name. He looked around for a moment; Celeste's ashes remained on the ground before him.

"Anastasia and I will bring you scraps to eat; you can leave at dusk."

. . .

As the sun began to drop below the treetops, Anastasia and her mother readied Donte for his long trip. They fed him scraps from dinner and a dozen apples, enough to hold him off until he went hunting.

Anastasia stood on her tiptoes and kissed Donte on the side of his nose; Tessa kissed him on the other side.

"I love you, Donte," Anastasia said.

Donte took to the sky and left behind the mother and daughter, along with the ashes of Celeste. He flew to the northeast, away from the barns, and headed toward Rickenback Mountain.

Once he reached the mountain, he circled over the western base. Grave markers of those who once resided in or around Ironwood spotted the grassy area.

He then flew due north. Once he soared over the Snake River, it was full night, and stars filled the sky. Off to the west, lightning intertwined within the clouds that hung over the Dark Forest. Every few seconds, the lightning illuminated the grounds of Evergreen. This light helped Donte hunt for his midnight snack.

. . .

The sun beat on his back when he reached the cabin the following day. He spotted Jake walking to the barns where the other dragons were. When his shadow crossed over the top of Jake, the man looked up and smiled. Donte landed where all the other dragons were, and they exchanged nose sniffs and grunts. Donte went over to where Ava rested. The old dragon looked up at him with weary eyes. It had been a few years since Donte had seen the matriarch of the dragons. He nudged some straw around her to help comfort her.

"Hello, Donte," Jake said from behind Donte.

Donte turned and looked at his original master. Jake walked to him, reached up, and patted him on the nose, "I'm sorry for what happened." Donte turned his head and looked off toward the mountains. Jake rubbed Donte's neck as he spoke, "We have to get you ready. You should eat, then you and Zelda will leave tomorrow at noon."

2

Jake equipped each dragon with a satchel around the neck. Zelda, the smallest of the dragons, stood next to Donte as Jake finished the preparations. Her eyes always mesmerized everyone; they looked as though someone had painted eyeliner around them. She was the smartest dragon of them all, and Donte was comforted by the fact that she would be next to him on this mission. Although Donte and Brutus were the strongest of the dragons, Zelda could scrap with any of them, and her brains made her a fiercer ally.

Jake commanded them off, and the two dragons took to the sky and headed toward the mountains. Donte flew high in the air and looked straight ahead; he knew what lay on the other side of the mountains. Zelda flew lower, scanning the ground for any trouble or perhaps a quick meal for her and Donte. They chased the sun through the sky as it neared the horizon. They had one mountain to clear before they reached Erikson's Castle.

Donte had anticipated reaching this point in the journey. He spent the flight remembering Celeste, thinking, wondering. As the last mountain grew nearer, his anger grew.

He remembered what happened that night. He and Celeste had slept in the barn. They stayed in the barn every night. Raistlin had grown concerned and wanted the dragons locked up in the evenings. Donte woke to a noise in the barn. A stranger stood before him, along with a man he knew, and then he was hit in the face with a sock full of powder. In seconds, he fell back asleep, remembering only the smell of patchouli that wafted off the two men.

When he woke, Celeste was still lying next to him. Her head leaned against him, so he scooted over, then her head rolled to the side. He realized she was dead; she had been decapitated. Since that moment, Donte had been in a daze.

He smelled the patchouli plants in the breeze as they cleared the final mountaintop. The lit sconces at the castle shimmered in the distance. Donte huffed in anger. Zelda slowed her flight and let Donte lead the way to the castle. Halfway down the mountainside, Donte heard a man scream, and he knew it was one of his friends. He and Zelda quickened their pace. Once they flew over the back gate, Zelda flew toward the ground and Donte flew toward the top of the castle. Donte spotted a woman at the back of the castle. She drew her bow and slung an arrow toward Zelda. He let out a burst of flame and disintegrated the arrow in mid-flight, the arrowhead tumbling through the air and bouncing off Zelda's wing. After the flame from the dragon, the woman retreated into the back of the castle.

Donte made his way to the top of a castle wall. A sword fight went on below him; two bodies lay on the ground in a pool of blood.

Donte stood on the top of the castle wall and let out a roar that shook the doors of the homes in Greystone. Along with the roar was a flame that shot out and singed the tops of the trees. Donte was furious; the anger that had built up in him over the past several weeks finally came to a head. He roared again, and it was even louder than the last one. The people of Greystone began fleeing their homes, screaming, and running away from the castle. Another flame shot out and burned more of the treetops.

Donte was given specific directions not to kill anyone or burn anything down. Jake gave him the speech before he and Zelda had departed for the castle.

Jake looked the dragon in the face. "No killing! Don't burn anything down!"

Donte looked off to his left.

"Donte! Look at me!" Jake raised his voice.

Donte looked back at him.

"Promise me!"

The dragon grunted and, as always, would obey an order from any one of his masters.

As he roared a third time, the top of the stone wall began to crumble under the tight grip of his claws.

He looked down and noticed that Dorn was one of the men engaged in the sword fight. If one of his masters were in grave danger, the rules didn't apply anymore. He leaned his head down to get a better look as his neck stretched below his feet. A knife sailed through the air and stuck into the back of the blond swordfighter. The man arched his back to try to reach the knife and staggered into the castle. Cambria appeared on the stone walkway from the left of Donte and ran toward the two men who were still fighting.

3

Dorn had never heard a dragon roar so loud in his life. The flames that Donte exhaled lit up everything like it was the middle of the day, and the heat was nearly unbearable. As Dorn engaged in the sword fight with Lance and the young blond, the young blond arched his back and let out a scream. He staggered his way back through an opening in the castle.

Dorn noticed a rare look of fear in Lance's eyes when Donte landed at the top of the castle wall and began roaring and breathing fire. Now that his fighting partner was out of the game, Lance began to backpedal. Dorn lurched forward with a barrage of attacks as Lance retreated. Lance fought the blows as he shuffled backward. Once his trench coat was beneath his feet where he had left it prior to the fight, he stooped down, grabbed the coat, and swung it over his head. He vanished in an instant.

Dorn took a few steps backward and looked around, cursing as Donte roared again, drowning out his rare lack of class.

Cambria ran up and kneeled next to Jared. Zelda, small enough to pass through the walkway between the castle and the curtain wall, followed close behind.

Dorn sheathed his sword as Cambria pulled items from inside her vest. Dorn ran to Zelda and sheathed Jared's sword into the leather strap that hung the satchel from the dragon's neck. He turned and kneeled next to Cambria.

Cambria tore strips of cloth covered in a white powder. She stuffed the cloth into Jared's chest. She pulled out more and kept stuffing it into his wound.

"Roll him over," Cambria yelled over Donte's constant roars.

Once Jared was on his stomach, she stuffed more cloth into the wound on his back. Dorn looked around for any danger as Cambria worked. Once she stopped the bleeding, she yelled to Zelda.

"Zelda! Here!"

Zelda approached, gently grabbed Jared with her jaws, and carried him to the courtyard behind the castle. Donte stopped his roaring and flew from the top of the castle wall into the courtyard to meet Zelda. As Dorn pulled a length of rope from Zelda's satchel, Zelda placed Jared onto the dragon. Cambria and Dorn worked quickly to tie Jared onto Donte's back. Once he was secure, Cambria climbed onto Zelda's back.

"Get on, Dorn. I think she can handle both of us," Cambria said.

Dorn looked back at the castle, "No, I'm staying."

"Dorn! You can't! Let's go!" Cambria pleaded.

Dorn looked up at the castle's tallest tower, "No, I have a score to settle. Go!"

"Dorn! You can't do this yourself!"

"I have to," Dorn said. "Donte, to the cabin! Zelda! Follow! Guard!"

At his command, the two dragons lifted off into the night sky and flew toward the mountains.

4

Cambria was furious when Dorn commanded the dragons to fly away. Tears welled in her eyes, some of them from the cool night air rushing at her face, the rest from anger.

Except for the occasional reflection of moonlight off Donte's scales, he blended into the night sky. He flew quickly, almost with a vengeance. Zelda worked to keep up.

A few hours later, they approached the barns and the cabin. Donte let out three long huffs as they flew over. Moments later, someone came out of the cabin with a lantern in hand.

Donte landed gently near the cabin. Zelda followed suit.

Cambria slid off Zelda, and once she reached Donte, she began loosening the ropes that held Jared. Jake set the lantern on the small deck and began to help.

"He's still alive. I stopped the bleeding," Cambria said.

Nana appeared in the doorway.

Once the ropes were cut loose, Cambria and Jake lowered Jared from the dragon. Zelda stepped forward and nudged Jared toward the cabin door as

Cambria and Jake struggled to carry him. Once they had him inside the door, Cambria relayed to Nana what she needed.

"Nana! Boil some water! I need turmeric, juniper root, and garlic!"

Cambria came out of the cabin door and pointed to Donte, "Go back and get Dorn! Go! Now!"

Without a snort, a huff, or a roar, Donte turned his head toward the mountains and took flight.

5

After the dragons took flight with Cambria and Jared in tow, Dorn hurried across the back courtyard and into the castle. The sight of the dragons just minutes earlier caused everyone to vanish. The castle was quiet. Wall sconces lit the corridors.

It was Dorn's first time in the castle, and he had never seen a map or drawing to help navigate the building. He had to find a way to get into the castle's tallest tower, but the corridors went in all directions like a maze. His boots scraped against the cobblestone floor as he walked. He lightened his steps to quiet them. The only other sounds were the flames whispering in their sconces.

"You there! Stop!" He heard a voice behind him.

Dorn stopped and slowly turned. A taller man approached. Although it was just a silhouette at first, a nearby sconce revealed his face. He had never seen the man before. Before the man spoke again, Dorn kicked his knee and heard a crack as it hyperextended.

The man fell to the ground, and he bellowed out a yell that echoed down the corridors.

Dorn moved faster through the castle, angry at himself for the loudness of the conflict. He heard a commotion as others came to the man's aid. One man ran around a corner and froze when he saw Dorn. The man directed Dorn to stop, then he stood in place, blocking the corridor.

Although he was armed with his sword at his side and his dagger tucked away in his leather vest, Dorn chose to fight with his hands. There was only one person in the castle he wanted to kill, and he hadn't reached his room yet.

Dorn took a swing and almost landed a perfect blow to the bigger man's jaw, but the man pulled his head back at the last moment. The man grabbed him, used the momentum from the punch, and threw him against the wall. The impact with the wall knocked the wind out of him. He gasped to try to get his breath back, and then the man swung at him. He blocked the punch and gave three quick jabs to his face. His opponent staggered backward and fell to the ground, dumbfounded.

Dorn jumped over the man and kept moving. Inside one archway a stairway went up, but he passed it up. A man guarded a second stairway. With a few quick moves, Dorn had the man on the ground.

He made his way up the stairway with the lightest of footsteps. The stairway went round and round as it ascended. Every time the stairway went a full circle, another sconce lit the way. Once the top of the stairway came into view, Dorn saw two men standing on the landing, guarding a door.

The men took a fighting stance, and one of them pulled a dagger. Dorn charged up the stone steps. His only choice was to take out their legs. Just as he lunged from the lower steps, the man without the dagger tried to kick Dorn in the head. As he turned to avoid the kick, Dorn reached up and grabbed the man by the waist of his pants and pulled, sending him tumbling down the steep stairway. Dorn jumped to his feet as the dagger from the other man swung at him. He turned away from the attack, but the knife grazed his arm, cutting through his shirt and the skin underneath. With the same arm that had been

12

sliced, Dorn gave a quick backhand to the nose. With blood running down his face, the man took another swipe with the knife. Dorn grabbed his wrist and slammed it down onto his knee, breaking a bone in the lower forearm. The dagger dropped from his hand, and it clanged down the stairs. Dorn pushed and the man tumbled down after the dagger, grunting and cursing as he went.

Dorn pushed the big wooden door, the hinges creaked as it slowly swung open. He stepped through the doorway and closed the slab of wood behind him.

The room was round with stone walls and a window on the side opposite the door. The floor was also constructed of stone. A fireplace was built in the wall on the left side, a fire blazing within. The room was warmer than any of the corridors. A rug on the floor stretched nearly to the walls.

Dorn dropped a wooden board across two hangers and secured the door shut. He took two steps toward the middle of the room where a bed lay. A tall candelabra stood at each corner of the bed with a candle burning in each brass base. Wax was built up on the sides of the candlesticks. His shadow danced back and forth on the wall to the right. He walked to the side of the bed with short, quiet steps. A man lay on the bed, his face old, pale, and sunken. Once Dorn reached the side of the bed, he could hear the shallow breathing from the old man; the only other sound in the room was the crackle of the fire.

The man on the bed was Ivan Erikson, Lance's father. Dorn looked down at the face and barely recognized him. Easy enough to understand, Dorn had only seen the man once. He had never forgotten the face after all the years; the man was just too old and sick to be recognizable. Dorn could remember the sound of his voice as well, "Go back! Go back and tell them what you saw! Run!" Those words rang in Dorn's head for decades, and he longed for this moment. One of the things he had wanted since that day was to kill the man who had murdered his father.

Now he stood over him at the edge of the bed. After every few shallow breaths, a rattle was heard from Ivan's chest. The man had a long gray beard and gray hair, the skin on his face pulled tight on his bony cheeks. His skin looked fragile, as if it would tear if Dorn simply touched Ivan's face with his fingers.

Dorn pulled his dagger from his leather vest. He ran his finger across the blade that was sharp enough to cut the width of a hair. The shiny blade shot reflections from the fire to the ceiling. Dorn shifted the dagger and held it in both hands close to his chest, the blade pointed down. He gripped the handle tighter and fought a frown as his anger began to rise. One swift lift of the blade over his head and down into Ivan's chest would end it all. He had envisioned this moment over and over since he was a child.

Just as he was about to commit the ultimate act of revenge, he slipped the knife back into his vest. He looked at Ivan, the death rattle could still be heard. Dorn pulled his vest down and flattened it out, then he crossed his hands at his waist as he glared at the man lying on the bed.

There was a commotion, then a banging. Then something smashed into the door, shaking it in the frame. It happened two more times and then the board that held the door shut splintered as the door flew open. The first man that Dorn had thrown down the stairs just moments before came tumbling through the doorway. Lance walked through the opening and stepped over the man. Brenna walked behind him.

Dorn didn't look up from his spot at the side of the bed. Lance and Brenna continued into the room, the man who busted through the door was now on his feet. Lance stopped and held out both of his hands and the two others stopped walking. The three stood and watched Dorn at the side of the bed. Dorn walked away from the bed as slowly as he had approached it minutes earlier. He walked toward the three, looking straight ahead. He stopped in front of the two men. He and Lance both stared straight ahead, not making eye contact.

"Let him pass," Lance said.

The big man who had earlier tumbled down the stairs obediently stepped aside. Dorn stepped forward to pass, and he and Lance bumped shoulders. Dorn stopped as both men faced opposite directions. Lance stood an inch taller than Dorn. The only sound they could hear was the crackle of the fire.

"This is over," Dorn mumbled.

Lance exhaled out of his nose and closed his eyes for a moment. When he opened them, Dorn was already walking down the circular staircase.

6

Dorn made his way through the castle and out onto the grounds. He peeked around the corner and looked for the little door that Raistlin and the boys had gone through, but it was gone. He crossed the back courtyard with no sign of Raistlin.

He walked through the back gate and stepped over one of the guards, who was still sound asleep. He started his long hike up the mountain. Many of the stars had faded due to the glowing morning sky that was developing in the east. As Dorn made his way up the mountain, the sounds of the crickets and cicadas faded,and the early morning was filled with the songs of Chiffchaffs, Goldfinches, and Bluebirds.

7

When Dorn made his way over the top of the mountain, the sun was rising in the distance. The tall grass was full of dew and the droplets sparkled in the sunlight. He held his hand up to block the light, and his breath was visible in the morning chill. Once his eyes adjusted, he saw the horns of a dragon poking from the grass. Through the tall grass, fierce green eyes looked at him.

Dorn stopped walking at the sight of Donte. The dragon blinked. Dorn took two steps forward and fell to his knees.

"Donte," he said. "Donte," a whisper this time. He held the palms of his hands to his eyes and tried to fight back tears. "Oh, buddy. I am so sorry." He fought sobs through gritted teeth as tears rolled down his cheeks. "I should have never locked you and Celeste in the barn. What was I thinking?" Finally, he sobbed, just a few times. Then he began wiping the tears from his face. "Can you forgive me, old friend?"

Donte moved his head closer to Dorn. Dorn held out his hands; Donte then put his chin on Dorn's knees. Dorn leaned forward and put his arms as far as he could around Donte's head. Donte grunted.

After a few moments, Dorn leaned back and looked at Donte. "What do you think? Time to head back?"

Donte grunted again and Dorn stood. Donte bumped him on the shoulder as his usual sign of affection. Dorn looked at the shoulder; he had forgotten about the cut from the guard at the top of the stairs. The shirt sleeve had a spot of blood the size of a fist, but the blood on the cut underneath was dry.

"Okay, let's go," Dorn said.

Donte leaned his head down for Dorn to climb on so they could fly.

"Not yet, buddy," Dorn said. "Let's just walk for a while."

Donte grunted and turned around so they could head east.

Once they began walking down the other side of the mountain, Dorn said, "What do you think? How about I go back and get the girl?"

8

Cambria worked through the night and into the morning trying to patch Jared's wounds. Jake helped her move him around as needed, and Nana provided an extra set of hands when she wasn't boiling water or mixing a concoction that Cambria had ordered. At one point, Jared began to scream as he neared consciousness. Cambria sprinkled slumber sand over his nose, and he quieted. Once she was done patching the wound from the front, the three of them gently flipped him over. She then unpacked the wound and checked for more bleeding. When she was satisfied, she poured one of the concoctions into the wound before she sewed it shut. Her arms were covered to the elbows with blood, and a red splotch adorned the front of her blouse.

When she was done, Jake rubbed her shoulders as they stood by the bed.

"Nice job, sweetheart," he said.

"Oh, he's lost so much blood," she said.

"All we can do is wait," he whispered.

9

Later that afternoon, Donte circled the cabin and landed in the open field with Dorn on his back. Cambria, Jake, and Nana were sitting on the back deck. Cambria was still in her bloody blouse, too tired to change her clothes.

Dorn slipped off the dragon and made his way to the deck. He stood in the grass and looked at the three sitting on the deck. He dropped his gaze to the ground and breathed a big sigh.

"He's lost a lot of blood," Cambria said.

Dorn opened his mouth for a moment, closed it, and then spoke, "You mean he's still alive?" he asked.

Cambria nodded, "Two dislocated ribs, two broken ribs, and a punctured lung. I had to cut a third of it out. Somehow the blade missed his heart and arteries."

"Will he make it?" Dorn asked.

Cambria shrugged, "I don't know." She stood up and whispered, "I don't know." Then she turned and went into the cabin.

Jake stood and walked to the edge of the deck. He looked out at the open area and watched as Donte tugged an apple out of a tree, then Jake walked down the steps and stood face to face with Dorn.

"Well?" Jake asked after searching Dorn's eyes.

Dorn looked down and shook his head, the corners of his mouth tugged toward the ground.

Jake, just slightly shorter than Dorn, stepped forward and put his arms around him. He whispered in his ear, "That's okay. There has been enough death." He hugged him harder, and Dorn returned the gesture. "Nana and I have loved you like you were our son, but nobody would be prouder of you than your father. He would be proud of you and everything you have ever done. You are a great man. I love you!"

Dorn squeezed harder and cried onto Jake's shoulder.

10

After two days at the cabin, Dorn bid his goodbyes and climbed up onto Donte to fly around the Dark Forest back to Barrow's Homestead.

The day after Dorn left, Jared was able to sit up in bed and eat chicken broth.

"Where's Raistlin?" he asked in a hoarse voice.

"We don't know," Cambria said as she sat on the edge of the bed. "He went through the door with the boys, then the door disappeared. Kind of like we thought it would, except I didn't expect you to still be here." She smiled at him.

Jared smiled back, then grimaced in pain and held his chest.

"Let me make you a tea for the pain," Cambria kissed him on the forehead.

"Why am I here?"

"You didn't make it out. Maybe The Great Fathers wanted it this way," she winked at him and walked into the kitchen.

. . .

Jared grew stronger as the days and weeks went by. They made plans: when he was strong enough, they would fly south to the homestead. Cambria had decided it was time to go back home, no more hiding at the cabin. She wasn't a kid anymore; she could take care of herself. It was time to quit hiding.

On the eve of leaving the cabin, their plans were thwarted. Jake walked into the cabin as Nana was cooking breakfast. He swept his gray hair to the side.

"I have sad news," he said and looked at the others. "Ava passed during the night."

They all stopped what they were doing.

"I'm sorry, Grandpa," Cambria said.

"She had a good life," he said. "I believe the other dragons are more broken hearted than we are. Let's eat, you two have to leave in the morning." Jake waved his hand toward the table for everyone to sit.

"Grandpa, we can stay for a few more days to help out," Cambria said. "We need to give her a good send off."

. . .

Brutus and Dorian dragged Ava away from the barn with ropes that were tied to her legs. Cambria and Jared raked the straw and sprinkled it around her. Jake chopped away at a fallen tree and put the logs into a wooden cart. Zelda pulled the cart back to where Ava's body lay. Cambria pulled the logs from the cart and stacked them around the dead dragon. Jared grabbed smaller chunks of wood, unable to lift much more than that.

They walked down to the barns after dinner as the sun began to set. All the dragons were gathered around, and when Jake, Nana, Cambria, and Jared approached, the dragons shuffled and took their places around Ava. The people stayed back, outside of the circle of dragons.

23

When the sun disappeared past the mountains and the first stars glowed in the sky, Jake said, "Okay, it's time."

Brutus scraped his right claw on the ground and huffed as he lowered his head. He let out a flame that doused the straw and logs that lay by Ava. The other dragons followed suit; Zelda, Dorian, and Alonzo all participated in the lighting. Alonzo was a little hesitant about what to do at first. He was still young and oblivious to some of the dragon's ways. Finally, as was ordinary for a pyre of a dragon, Brutus held his head back and roared into the dusk, a roar to let the next world know that a dragon was coming. The people of the group held their hands to their ears; Alonzo even stepped back for a moment. The roar was so loud it shook the ground and, as they noticed when they returned later, vibrated things off the shelf and onto the floor of the cabin.

The flames of the pyre reached into the evening sky. The colors changed from orange to purple, then a golden color appeared. As they watched the fire, the colors constantly changed, and sparks glowed into the sky as far as they could see. There was no anger this time, unlike when Celeste died. They watched the beauty of the fire as Ava's body slowly turned to ash. After some time, Jake pulled out his fiddle and played a slow, sad song.

Cambria stood with her hand tucked in the crook of Jared's arm, and when Jake was done with the song, she whispered in Jared's ear, "We're having a baby."

He looked at her, looked away, then looked back again. He put his arm around her waist, kissed her on the lips, and they watched the embers from the pyre float into the night sky.

11

Donte always let out a huff to let anyone know he was approaching. He circled and landed at his usual spot just down the slope of Raistlin's yard. Anastasia came running out of the house with her curly hair bouncing behind her as Dorn slid off the dragon. She sprinted and jumped into Dorn's arms.

"Dorn, where's Daddy?" she asked as she looked around.

"He's going to be a while, sweetheart," he said as he kissed her on the cheek.

"Hi, Donte," she said as she patted the dragon on the nose. "Dorn," she was whispering this time, "don't tell Mommy, but I'm going to give Donte some eggs because I missed him."

"What about me? I don't get any eggs?" Dorn whispered back as he walked her to the house.

"Mommy makes you eggs all the time."

Tessa came out of the house and stood on the porch as Dorn approached. Dorn let Anastasia down and looked at Tessa, not sure what to say.

"Anastasia, go in and get your stuff ready so we can go to the shop." Once Anastasia was inside, Tessa looked back at Dorn, "Did the boys make it home?"

"Yes, well, Josh and Billy did." Dorn studied her face, a breeze blew a lock of brown hair across her cheek. "Jared was hurt bad, but he is going to be okay."

"Raistlin?"

"He's gone. He took the boys through the door but couldn't get back." He looked down and swept at some grass with his boot, then looked back up. "I'm going to have to meet with The Great Fathers and see what their plan is. I'll find him."

12

Dorn went to Ironwood later that afternoon and walked into the saloon. He nodded to a few others and then sat at the bar. Sally came walking from the other end of the bar.

"Well, look who's here. It's been a while," she said.

Dorn let a small grin escape, and when she leaned over the bar to receive her usual kiss on the cheek, he kissed her on the lips.

She backed up for a second, then smiled. She reached behind the bar for a bottle of whiskey and a glass and set them on the bar in front of Dorn. "Well, it's about time," she said and winked at him.

. . .

Dorn watched the sky every night as the three moons came closer and closer to alignment.

13

Zelda flew with a small amount of cargo strapped to her back. She trailed Dorian as they approached the homestead. The bigger dragon had Jared and Cambria as cargo.

The excitement of Cambria and Jared coming home was compounded by the news that Tessa was about to become a grandmother and that Anastasia was about to become an aunt.

"Does your father know?" Tessa asked Cambria.

"No, we didn't know 'til after he left," Cambria said.

"He is going to be so excited," Tessa said as she hugged Cambria.

Cambria's baby bump was barely noticeable when they had arrived at the homestead, but it seemed to grow by the day.

14

Jared walked with Dorn up the hill, and they stopped by the big boulders and the pines. Jared was winded from losing part of a lung from his injuries.

"I have never done this," Dorn said as he looked up at the moons.

"It must be an honor," Jared said.

"I have waited decades for this," Dorn grabbed the lantern from the top of the boulder and sighed. "I'll see you in a bit," he said and walked through the pines.

His lantern lit the cave as he entered. It looked just as Raistlin had described over the years.

Raistlin was the chosen one to be able to meet with The Great Fathers when the three moons, The Dragon Moon, The Prophet's Moon, and The Traveler's Moon, all aligned. Now that Raistlin was gone, Dorn was the one to meet with the men who knew the secrets of Evergreen

He sat on the Bubinga bench that Raistlin had told him about. He had no idea who made it, but it was beautiful. Dorn, a handy craftsman, had never seen Bubinga in Evergreen. He had no idea where it came from or how it ended up in the cave.

He looked up and saw the hook on the wall; he reached up and hung his lantern from it.

Across the cave, a dim light appeared in the tunnel. The light grew brighter, then a man walked out holding a lantern. Dorn stood. His heart swelled in his chest.

"Father," Dorn whispered.

"Hello, son," Dominic Hale stood across the small stream from Dorn.

Dorn wanted to leap across the stream and throw his arms around his father, but that is just something that couldn't be done. Dorn dropped to his knees. He was at a loss for words.

"I am so sorry, Son," Dominic said as he squatted down and looked across the stream at Dorn.

"No, I'm sorry, Daddy. I wish I could have done something."

"You were young. It was all my fault; I was taking a risk. It never should have happened," Dominic said. "There are good things we can talk about. It sounds like you have been a good man to the Barrow family."

"They are the best people in Evergreen. I would do anything for them."

"Jake was a great friend; you were left in good hands. How is he?"

"He is wonderful. Just living off the land at the cabin," Dorn said.

"Yes, of course," Dominic said.

Footsteps were heard shuffling in the tunnel and Randall Barrow walked into the cave, his long gray hair and beard draped over his robe.

He looked startled when he saw the two other men, "Oh, I came too soon. My apologies, gentlemen."

"It's okay, sir. Stay," Dorn said.

Randall stepped forward and patted Dominic on the back and nodded at Dorn. "My," Randall said. "I haven't seen you since you were a baby."

"I have heard nothing but good things about you, sir," Dorn said.

30

Randall nodded. The third of The Great Fathers came into the cave, also holding a lantern. This man was younger than any of them and shorter as well.

"Hello, gentlemen," Asmund Edmund said. Then he looked at Dorn, "Hello, Dorn."

"Sir," Dorn said, his dark eyes gleaming in admiration for the man he had never met, but had heard legends about.

"Shall we get started?" Asmund said.

The three men nodded and shuffled to their respective benches.

15

What was an emotional greeting just moments before was now a serious meeting amongst men. Dorn slid forward on his bench; his dark eyes were cold.

"How did they know we were coming?" Dorn asked. "We did everything, took all the precautions. We spied on them several times. They were supposed to be on a hunting outing."

Asmund sat up straighter on his bench, "Forces are working against us."

Dorn glared at him, "What does that mean?"

Randall Barrow spoke, "We cannot just call the shots, we can only guide you. We can tell you what doors are open, or what may happen; after that, it is out of our control." He leaned back and flattened his long beard against his chest.

"Raistlin could have been killed," Dorn said, the pitch of his voice a little higher than normal. "And Jared never got out!"

"We understand your frustrations, Son," Dominic said.

Dorn dropped his head and was quiet for a moment, then he said, "Of course, Father."

"But, there is a plan," Asmund said.

Dorn looked up.

"As you know, Raistlin is not in Evergreen," Asmund folded his hands on his lap.

Dorn nodded, "Yes, the door he and the boys went through disappeared."

"We know where you can find him," Asmund looked Dorn in the eyes. "You will have to travel for it."

"Where to?" Dorn asked.

"Out of Evergreen," Asmund said.

"Out of Evergreen?" Dorn glared at him.

Asmund continued, "You'll have to take Jared with you, he will be able to navigate the other world better than you. Things are very advanced there, you'll see." Asmund lightly scratched one side of his short, well-kept beard. "You will also have to take Billy Blaine with you."

Dorn's face went blank. "Billy?" He asked. "He's gone."

Asmund nodded, "Yes, he is gone. But he is coming back soon. You, Jared, and Billy must go to Billy's hometown, the place he grew up."

16

The following week, Sally was elected mayor of Ironwood. As a well-respected woman, the proprietor of the saloon, and the landlord of the blacksmith's shop and the adjoining house, it was an easy vote for her to win. The townspeople viewed her as one who wanted to improve the town in the best interests of the citizens as opposed to benefiting herself or her own prosperity.

Three days after the election win, Dorn asked Sally to marry him while they were on horseback overlooking the small valley outside of Ironwood. They decided that on the next Day of the Feast, they were to be married.

17

The day the Dragon Moon is to be full, the people from Ironwood and the surrounding area all gather in the open field and prepare food and campsites for a fun-filled afternoon and evening called the Day of the Feast. Children help with whatever needs to be done, knowing full well that later in the day they will have fun, games, and maybe even the possibility of a show from the dragons, and surely the opportunity to pet them.

Fires were made early in the day and tents were erected. Pots of stew with smoked sausage, cabbage, carrots, onions, green beans, corn, potatoes, and ham hocks began to steam, filling the air with a wonderful aroma. Pies were baked in makeshift outdoor ovens. Wood fire pits had been lit early to grill deer steaks and chicken. Barrels of ale were rolled out, and bottles of whiskey were placed at the tables. The Day of the Feast was more than just a gathering with food and good times; it was a bond throughout the community. It was a show of love and trust; it was an opportunity to set differences aside. Two men involved in a saloon fight the prior evening would shake hands and act like old pals during the Day of the Feast.

Dorn stirred a large pot of chili, one of Sally's family recipes. Jared stood on the other side of the fire that warmed the chili.

"Big day today," Jared said.

"Yes," Dorn said as he held a spoonful of chili under his nose for a sniff. "I'm glad you are here to be a part of it."

"I wouldn't miss it for the world."

"Why don't you join us? I know you want to marry Cambria. We can make it a double wedding." Dorn dumped the contents of the spoon back into the pot.

"Not today," Jared said as he looked across the field. "I don't want to steal your thunder."

"I don't bring thunder."

Jared's eyes met Dorn's, "Yes you do. In a good way."

"Well," Dorn said. "I'm glad you think so."

The two men stood in a trance for a moment, but then it was interrupted when Donte stood in the distance and huffed. Dorn looked over and Donte had his head raised to the sky, slightly confused.

Only a dragon knows when a new arrival in Evergreen is about to happen. Whether it's something in the air, or they can just feel a person shifting between two parallel worlds, somehow they sense that it is about to happen.

With Dorn's knowledge of dragons, and his information from the Great Fathers, he knew something special was about to happen. He set the big wooden spoon on a rock and yelled, "Everyone! Please gather! Quickly!"

All chores were put on hold for a moment, and everyone rushed to the gravel area at the bottom of the hill. Sally, who had been making some rounds with the townspeople, joined Dorn. Jared pulled Cambria up from a nearby chair, and they held hands for the short walk.

Everyone lined each side of the gravel lane. Donte continued to look one way, then the other, to figure out what was happening.

Jared leaned towards Dorn, "What's going on?"

36

Dorn looked at him and smiled, "You'll see."

Up the hill, a yell could be heard, a happy yell, the yell of a young boy. Jared turned his head and glanced at Dorn. Dorn gave the tiniest nod and a small smile.

Then Billy Blaine appeared at the bottom of the hill, running at a full sprint. This was the same path Billy had taken so many times as he and Dorn worked with the dragons in the past. Billy skidded to a halt in the stones.

A voice from the far end of the group bellowed, "Ladies and Gentlemen, hailing from Dee-troit, Michigan, Mister Billy Blaine!"

The townspeople erupted in cheers. Anastasia and Tessa were near Dorn, Sally, Cambria, and Jared; Anastasia jumped up and down and yelled, "Billy Blaine! Billy Blaine!"

Donte stepped forward and leaned his head over a part of the group; he sniffed Billy, then, with the blow of a nostril, blew the Detroit Tigers cap off Billy's head. The crowd roared with laughter.

"Donte," Billy exclaimed.

Anastasia ran up and kissed Billy on the cheek and whispered, "I love you, Billy Blaine." Then she ran back to her mother.

Billy wore the same overalls that Tessa had made for him, and he had tennis shoes on his feet. When Billy met Dorn's eyes, Dorn gave him a polite salute. Billy looked to the right of Dorn and saw Jared and Cambria.

"You two are going to have a baby," Billy said.

Jared and Cambria looked at each other and laughed.

"Josh isn't here?" Billy asked.

Jared shook his head, "Not yet."

Billy looked down for a second, "No, I reckon not."

Billy looked through the crowd as if he was searching for someone. Then he looked back in the direction of Dorn and Jared and asked, "Where's Raistlin?"

37

Dorn and Jared glanced at each other, then Dorn spoke, "We haven't seen him yet, Billy. But, I am glad you are here. You, Jared, and I have a trek to take, to search for Raistlin."

Jared looked back at Dorn, one side of his mouth formed a small grin.

18

When dusk settled in, Theodore Johnson walked to the main bonfire in the middle of the feast grounds. Raistlin was normally the current Chaplain of Ironwood, which was typical for one chosen to communicate with The Great Fathers. Dorn would have been the next in line, but since he was the one getting married, Theodore had to step in.

Theodore Johnson was a round, burly man who was much less intimidating once a person got to know him. He had an unkept beard that pulled to the sides like a Butterfly Bush that had grown out of control. During a drunken saloon fight that had gotten too rowdy, Theodore threw a patron out of the sixteen-lite front window. He hadn't done it in anger. His only reason was that the fight had gotten to the point that Sally couldn't handle it. The next day he helped Dorn replace the saloon window, and then later that afternoon he went to the house of the man he tossed out the window and helped him weed his garden.

"Ladies and gents," he bellowed when he reached the fire, all the townspeople stayed in their seats at their campfires, which was usual in an event like this. "The Day of the Feast is always a special day, but today is extra special. Today we get to celebrate the unity of two people in love. Our beloved mayor,

Sally Jenkins, and the great Dorn Hale will be united in marriage tonight." The crowd cheered; children jumped up and down on their benches. "I would ask the wonderful couple to approach the fire," Theodore said.

Another round of cheers came from the crowd as Sally and Dorn walked to the open area toward the big fire, their hands laced together.

When they reached the fire, Theodore said, "In the tradition of Evergreen, you each get to choose one to stand for you. Any person, young or old." He turned his head toward Sally, "Sally, you choose first."

Sally turned to the gathering in the field, "I choose Anastasia Barrow."

Everyone cheered as Anastasia ran toward the couple, a huge smile on her face. She slowed once she reached the clearing and stood next to Sally.

Theodore turned to Dorn, "Mr. Hale?"

"I choose," Dorn paused for a moment. "From Dee-troit, Michigan, Mr. Billy Blaine."

The crowd cheered again; Billy made his way toward the fire with a confident walk. Once he reached the circle of light that the fire emitted, Anastasia held her hands to her mouth and giggled. Billy stood as tall as he could next to Dorn.

"So, here we stand this evening, closing out another Day of the Feast. A day when we come together as one and put our differences aside. When we cook food for each other even though we are not in a time of need. When we share a drink with a neighbor and talk about things that make us smile. When all of this happens, the days that follow are brighter than ever, and morale for Ironwood and the surrounding area is restored. The Great Fathers must smile as they watch over these gatherings." Theodore looked over the field; campfires danced in the dusk. "Just when we think the day couldn't get better, we have the unity of two wonderful people. Two people that have given to this town and this community, two people that would do anything for anyone here, two people that I am honored to call my friends." He bowed his head slightly, "Ladies and gentlemen, Dorn Hale and Sally Jenkins."

The people cheered.

"To live in Evergreen means to live a simple life, and our unity ceremonies are simple as well." The man looked down at Anastasia. "Anastasia," he said.

Anastasia nodded with a cute smile.

"Anastasia, do you accept the fact that Dorn and Sally will be united?"

"Yes sir, I do," she said.

The man turned to Billy, "William, do you accept the unison of Dorn and Sally?"

Billy looked at Dorn and Sally before returning his gaze to the man, "I am honored to, sir."

"Then The Great Fathers shall recognize it as so. Ladies and gentlemen, when I introduce the new couple, I expect a cheer for all of Evergreen to hear, meet Mr. and Mrs. Dorn and Sally Hale!"

The crowd erupted as Dorn and Sally kissed. Kids pumped their arms in the air, and adults clinked their beer mugs together. As if accepting a challenge from the roar of the crowd, all of the dragons roared at once.

When the five of them faced the people, a few glowing objects floated into the air. First, there were just a handful of them, then a dozen, then several dozen. The small contraptions made from willow twigs and light pieces of cloth were fueled by a wick that had been soaked in oil. Now nearly a hundred of them floated into the night sky. The objects floating in the sky were an extra project that was put together by several families involved in the feast. They looked like miniature hot air balloons. Many of them had different patterns in the cloth that wrapped the flexible willow twigs, making the sky light up with many different colors.

Anastasia gasped when she saw them, "Look, Billy, look!" She pointed. Even those who helped construct the floating decorations were amazed at the beauty of the event.

19

Later that evening, after most of the campfires were snuffed out and the townspeople had gone home, Jared and Cambria were married in a quiet ceremony held by Theodore. Dorn and Sally stood for the couple since all the others had gone to bed. When the quick ceremony was finished, Dorn told them to close their eyes. He shuffled around for a moment, and the sound of striking flint was heard.

"Okay, open your eyes and turn around," Dorn said.

An object that stood about as high as Dorn's knee looked just like all the floating art projects that had lit the sky earlier in the evening. This one had a small rag bundled at the bottom, the rag burned, and the object slowly lifted off the ground. The flame grew bigger, and the object drifted over their heads. Sally had wrapped it with a beautiful, colorful cloth she had bought from Tessa's shop. As the flame flickered, the colors on the side danced as it floated over the treetops.

"Beautiful," Cambria whispered.

. . .

The next day, Sally and her bloodhound, Lulu, moved in with Dorn. Dorn's house was a small log cabin with two bedrooms. An oak table and chairs adorned the kitchen with a wood stove to cook, but the woodstove hadn't been used in years. Dorn typically ate almost every meal down the hill at Raistlin's house, or occasionally he would grab a sandwich at the saloon. Marrying Sally was a huge change in his life, he wasn't sure how to handle all of it. Once Sally's things were in place, they swept the wooden floor of the spare bedroom, put new linens on the bed, and let Billy stay.

. . .

A few days later, after Dorn rode with Sally to the saloon, he came back and found Jared doing stretches on the lawn in Raistlin's yard.

"How's the recovery?" Dorn asked as he slipped off Cherokee and tied the reins to a tree.

"Getting better," Jared said. "I'm sore, but Cambria babies me and won't let me do the things I want to yet."

"You should listen to her, she knows."

"Yeah, I know." Jared held out his hand and Dorn helped him to his feet. "So, what's the latest?" Jared asked.

Dorn thought for a moment, "Ivan Erikson is dead. The Great Fathers told me he passed a few nights ago." Dorn took a deep breath and closed his eyes.

Jared was silent for a moment, then said, "I don't know what to say, Dorn."

Dorn patted him on the shoulder, "You always know what to say, my friend."

Jared gazed down at the barns, where the two dragons were pulling apples from the high branches and dropping them down for Anastasia and Billy to collect. "What's this trek you spoke of when Billy came back?"

"Up at the top of the hill," Dorn nodded toward the hill that overlooked the grounds of the Day of the Feast. "There will be a door. We have to go and find Raistlin. You have to go with me because you will know the ways of the world we go to. Billy has to go because it's his hometown."

"How long will we be?"

"We don't know," Dorn said. "Time is different there, at least that is what Raistlin has told me."

"You've never...?"

Dorn shook his head before Jared could continue.

"So, we are going into this thing," Jared paused for a moment. "Blind?"

Dorn nodded.

"That door?" Jared asked. "Will that be on the rock wall?'

Dorn nodded again.

"There was a bear in the cave when we came out of that door; Raistlin, Josh, and me."

"May not be the case. Different scenarios. The Great Fathers work with other forces to make this happen."

"When do we leave?" Jared asked.

"When the Traveler's Moon is full."

20

They packed their bags for the trip; Jared recommended traveling light. If they were going to Billy's hometown, they wouldn't be doing much wilderness travel, and he didn't want them to draw attention with big backpacks. Billy put the few clothes he felt he needed into the leather backpack Raistlin had made for him just before their trek through the Dark Forest. As Dorn was packing a small pack, Jared handed him a purple book.

Dorn's eyes widened, "Where did you get this?"

"I stole it out of my brother's pack while we camped at the top of the mountain the night before the fight with Lance," Jared said. "I had a feeling I wasn't going to make it back home, and thought maybe you or Raistlin would need it at some point." He paused for a moment as he checked the things in his own pack, "It's the first time I had ever taken anything from him."

Dorn nodded, "I'm sure he would understand."

"I hope so," Jared said as he tied his pack shut.

. . .

46

The purple light from the Traveler's Moon left the landscape with a lazy hue. Billy walked with Jared and Dorn up the hill to the stone wall. He felt like an adult again, walking with two of the greatest men he had ever met. He was excited to go on this trek and knew how important it was to get Raistlin back home.

A wooden door was mounted at the base of the rock wall. It looked just like the one Billy, Josh, and Raistlin had crawled through for Josh and Billy to get back home.

Dorn turned and looked out through the trees across the land. "Well," he said and looked at Jared, "Ready?"

Jared nodded, "Yeah, let's do this."

Dorn looked down at Billy, who was also looking through the trees, "Billy?"

Billy tightened the straps on his pack, "Ready as I'll ever be."

Dorn nodded, "Okay then. Let's go."

Dorn pulled the door open; it was dark on the other side. He motioned for Jared to go first. Jared got on his hands and knees and crawled through, then Billy followed. Finally, Dorn crawled through and pulled the door shut behind him.

21

They were in a long corridor, the only light came from the far end. They walked toward the light, drips of water falling into a puddle could be heard over their light steps. The corridor became brighter the further they walked. About halfway to the end, Dorn pointed to something lying near the wall.

Jared walked over, picked up a white bag, and looked inside. He pulled out a cellular phone.

"What's that?" Dorn asked.

"Modern-day communication device," Jared said as he continued to dig through the bag. Next, he pulled out a leather wallet. He opened it and ran his thumb across dozens of twenty-dollar bills. Out of one of the little pockets in the wallet, he pulled out a driver's license. He looked at it and saw a picture of himself, it was the same picture as the ID while he was in the military, except this was a Michigan-issued driver's license, not an Ohio one. He tried to see the issue date on the license, but it was still too dark. There was a credit card in the slot next to the driver's license. He folded the wallet and slid it into his pocket; he placed the cell phone in the other pocket.

They resumed walking to the end of the corridor, as they got closer, they could see the daylight shining through an archway. Once they reached the end of the corridor, the three of them stood under the stone archway and looked out.

The stone arch was located at the edge of a copse of trees. Curvy concrete paths weaved in and out of the landscaping. The three of them took a few steps forward to get out of the trees for a better look at the surroundings. A river flowed to the left, and before them was a city skyline. In the foreground was a large parking garage with tall buildings jutting into the sky behind it. It was hot and humid, nothing like the weather in Evergreen.

"Billy, this is Detroit," Jared said.

"I'm guessing if Josh was here, he'd say, 'Thanks, Mr. Obvious,'" Billy said, his grin showing the gap in his front teeth.

"You were a nice kid once, Billy. Then you met my brother."

"Awe, shucks," Billy looked up at him with a worried look.

Jared smiled and rubbed Billy's shoulder.

Billy felt better immediately. He stepped forward and looked around. He pointed to the tall buildings closest to the river. "Those are the GM buildings; Corktown is on the other side of those." He moved his finger to the right, "The Tigers play over there on the other side of those buildings."

"Tigers?" Dorn asked.

"It's a professional sports team," Jared said. "They play baseball. Josh and I grew up as fans." Then he added, "Billy too, but different players in his time."

Billy turned around and faced the river, "There is an island over there on the river. That's where I proposed to- hey wait!" He leaned his head to look through the trees. "What happened to the archway we just walked through?"

The other two turned around, and the three of them stood and looked at trees, concrete riverwalks, grass, and a river; the stone arch was gone.

"I guess that's how it works," Jared said. He turned and faced the city again. "Shall we?"

"Yes," Dorn said.

"Can I see the book?" Jared asked.

Dorn reached into a side pocket of his pack and pulled out the purple book.

Jared grabbed it and opened it, "Nothing." He handed the book back.

Billy pointed again, "I grew up in Corktown."

"Then lead the way, my friend," Dorn said.

The three of them walked toward the city in search of their friend.

The year was 2022.

Part II: Raistlin

Raistlin sat with his head in his hands long enough for his shadow to move from his left side to his right. When he looked up, the arches for Josh and Billy were gone; there was just a rock wall. The absence of the arches meant the boys made it home.

Raistlin knew it had been a long shot to get Jared home. That was a task that was even out of the hands of The Great Fathers. The purpose was to get the boys home, something he knew he could do. He knew it came with sacrifice; he knew it wasn't guaranteed for all of them to make it out unscathed. It was worth the risk. He had nothing to do with Billy, Josh, and Jared winding up on his doorstep, but he made sure he had everything to do with trying to get them back home.

Now, Jared had a wound that was likely mortal. Then Raistlin had to leave Dorn behind to fight, and he knew his daughter, Cambria, was close behind. If Dorn went to the fight, she would show as well. Now Raistlin sat in the In Between with no idea how any of them fared.

Lance's In Between was destroyed because of his own carelessness. Regardless, the In Between was always there, in some way. The In Between had to be there, and had been there since the creation of Evergreen. There had to be a path to and from the real world, the real world where everyone from Evergreen originally came from.

Some people were born in Evergreen, and others just showed up. Some people remembered their life in the real world, others had vague visions of their previous life, and some had no recollection at all. Raistlin was born in Evergreen and had a vague idea of his previous life. Dorn was also born in Evergreen, but he had no recollection of his previous life. Anastasia was born in Evergreen, and Billy told her she had a previous life, but she never recalled any of it.

After all his years in Evergreen, he didn't think much about the past; he was too focused on making things better and doing the right thing. Now, here he sat, alone in the In Between.

Earlier, when the boys walked to their arches, the trees around Raistlin were just starting to bud. Now, when he looked up from where he sat on the ground, the trees had blossomed; white flowers adorned some of the trees, blues and purples for the others. He sat on a low-grade slope with trees all around him. Perpendicular to where he sat, a grass strip cut through, and there were trees on the other side that stood before the rock wall. Those trees had blossomed as well, some of them looked like branches full of snow.

Raistlin stood, stretched, and walked down the low grade onto the grass. The sun was warm on his skin; he held his face to the sky and closed his eyes, wondering what he was about to face.

After a moment, he opened his eyes and lowered his head; a slight breeze swept through the small valley and pulled a lock of his salt and pepper hair over his shoulder. Before him, nothing had changed, just trees with new flower

52

blossoms and a stone wall. He looked to his left, grass extended as far as he could see. To his right, in the distance, three men stood with their robes flowing in the wind.

The Great Fathers, Asmund Edmund, Randall Barrow, and Dominic Hale, stood in the grass, looking at Raistlin. Meetings with The Great Fathers always took a serious tone, but when Raistlin saw the look in the eyes of the three men, he knew this was a greater issue than he had ever dealt with.

The Great Fathers turned and walked away from Raistlin; Raistlin followed. The grass grew taller as they walked; the rock walls on each side of them grew closer together as well. The terrain became rocky and gradually dropped down in a long, stairstep fashion. Water dripped down the steps as Raistlin followed the men. Soon, the drips became a trickle as the steps leveled out; a small stream began to appear as they traveled. The Great Fathers walked on the left side of the stream, and Raistlin went to the right. They kept walking, and the stream grew to a few feet wide. The rock wall on Raistlin's side widened out into a horseshoe shape. Along the curved rock wall, arches stood, one after the other. All the trees now had their white, blue, and purple blossoms falling to the ground.

The men on the opposite bank stopped walking. Raistlin stopped with them, and they faced one another.

Asmund refocused his eyes on a spot behind Raistlin. Raistlin looked over his shoulder at an arch, then back at the men. Asmund nodded.

Raistlin walked to the arch; beyond the opening was complete darkness. He walked forward and passed through the opening. Once he was inside, it brightened up, and the world outside seemed to darken like it was dusk.

Around him, it lit up like a stage in a Broadway play. Lance was the center of the scene; he had Brenna and Boris, his blond swordfighter, with him. They were in the saloon in Greystone, a saloon Raistlin hadn't entered since he was a little kid with his father. Lance was standing and laughing. Boris and another man joined the laughter. Raistlin remembered Boris from the swordfight at the castle and numerous other run-ins with Lance, but he didn't recognize the other man with the long brown hair and tattoos. Brenna sat on a barstool with a grin on her face. A drunk man barely sat on the middle stool at the bar. Lance was yelling at the man and laughing. Raistlin couldn't decipher what was being said. The man could hardly balance himself on the stool. He wore worn-out clothing, and his hair was dirty and disheveled. Lance yelled something at the man, then kicked his stool out from under the man, causing him to hit his head on the bar and go down. Lance held his head back and howled with laughter. He then helped the man to his feet and sat him on another stool. The man held his hand to his head, blood slowly seeping through his fingers. Then Lance kicked the stool out from under him, sending him spilling to the floor again.

"Leave him alone," Raistlin yelled.

No one in the saloon paid attention.

Raistlin yelled again and realized it was useless. He walked out of the cave; the trees were full of leaves; all the blossoms were gone. He looked at The Great Fathers; Asmund nodded to the second archway.

Raistlin entered this archway and it brightened to an outside evening scene. Lance and Boris stood outside a home; Lance banged on the door. After a moment a man answered the door in his bedtime clothes. The man had a surprised look on his face when he saw who was calling.

"No," the man said, holding his hands out. "No, please, no. I'll do anything, just don't take my son!"

Lance pulled the man out of the doorway. Boris roughed the guy up with a few blows to the abdomen with his fists. Lance entered the house, and a lady screamed. Lance then walked out of the house, dragging a boy in nightclothes behind him. The boy cried and dragged his feet as Lance pulled him along.

"What are you doing?" Raistlin yelled from the shadows.

Lance dragged the boy and walked right by Raistlin; Boris followed. None of them noticed Raistlin.

Raistlin stormed out of the arch and walked toward the stream. "What is going on here?" He yelled. The leaves on the trees were the mixed colors of autumn, and many of them were falling to the ground. The air was slightly cooler than it had been just moments before.

None of the men answered his question. Asmund nodded to the third archway.

Raistlin hesitated a moment, then went to the arch and entered. He was in a long room, single beds adorned each side. Kids, all young boys, stood at attention at the ends of their beds. Lance walked down the aisleway, scowling at each boy as he passed. He stopped in front of one boy and began yelling at him, Raistlin couldn't make out the words. Lance then pushed the boy to the floor and spun around to the boy on the other side of the aisle. He yelled something and slapped that boy across the face.

Raistlin raced forward, "I've seen enough, Lance!" he said.

Lance didn't respond; he just continued to yell at the boy.

Raistlin raised his fist when he reached Lance and heaved a haymaker at him. It was a beautiful punch, right on the button, but Raistlin's punch never connected. He hit nothing but air. It would have landed right on Lance's chin, but it went through Lance's face like he wasn't there. Raistlin swung again, this one would have landed on Lance's left ear, but Raistlin's fist went right through his head. Lance went on like Raistlin wasn't even there. Raistlin swung a few more times and realized swinging at Lance didn't do anything more than yelling did.

He stomped out of the arch, his face red with anger.

"What is this?" he screamed.

The Great Fathers stood stone-faced as Raistlin approached the stream. The trees were bare, and snow was falling from the sky; the temperature had dropped considerably.

"Why are you showing me this? That's not real." Raistlin said in a loud voice as he pointed toward the arches behind him, his breath a vapor in the cold air.

"It's real," his grandfather said. "It was all real. We thought you should know."

Raistlin was dumbfounded. "How long has Lance been treating his people this way?"

The question wasn't answered. The men stood without a word.

Raistlin turned around to the arches. There was still one he hadn't entered.

"The last arch is for you," Dominic's bellowing voice was dulled by the wind that had just picked up. "This will take you where you are going."

Raistlin turned back to the men, "Where am I going?"

"Dorn will come and find you," Asmund said.

"Where am I going?" Raistlin asked again.

The men stood stoic. "That path leads you where you need to go," Asmund said.

Raistlin turned, and the horseshoe of arches was gone. Now there was a straight wall with one big archway. Raistlin turned back around, but the men were gone. There was just a stream and a stone wall.

23

A torch on the wall lit the tunnel Raistlin had just entered. Raistlin walked by the torch but then turned back and pulled it off its base from the wall. He held it off to his side as he walked. The tunnel was built entirely of stone; water drips could be heard, and from time to time, a drop of water landed on his head. He continued to walk, only being able to see as far as the torch would allow.

After what seemed like hours, Raistlin held the torch high; it looked as though there was a wall ahead, putting a dead end to the tunnel. He walked closer to it and confirmed that the tunnel was indeed ending. He didn't understand, there were no side tunnels or forks to decide which way to go, just a straight tunnel. He would have to turn back. He raised his torch over his head; up ahead of him, the floor dropped out. At the base of the wall, there was a void in the floor.

Raistlin walked to the void, held his torch high above his head, and looked down. It was a shaft that went straight down. He could see light at the bottom. He leaned forward and lost his balance; he slipped on the surface on which he had been walking. His torch fell from his hands as he scrambled for hold. He waved his arms to try to regain his balance; he could hear the torch bounce off the sides of the shaft as it fell. His balancing act was of no help and he fell. The light at the bottom was blue water. He fell so fast it was as if the pool of water rushed up to meet him.

He landed on his side, but water still rushed up his nose. He opened his eyes and tried to find his way to the surface. The water was warmer than the air he had just fallen through. His head broke the surface and he coughed several times. The bottom of the body of water was blue sand which gave off a blue glow to the cave he was in. Four torches, one in each compass direction, hung from the cave walls. He swam to the edge and walked out of the water. He realized his sword was gone. He had no idea where he left it, but he still had his dagger.

He brushed his hair back and squeezed some of the water out. The air was cold on his wet skin. Next to one of the torches was a tunnel, the only one in the cave.

He walked to the tunnel and pulled the torch from the wall. Just inside the tunnel, he found a pile of clothes folded on the floor. He pulled a heavy coat off the top and looked at it, then at the flannel shirt that was next on the pile. He set the torch on the floor of the tunnel and began stripping off his wet clothes. First went the leather vest, then the white cotton shirt, then his leather boots and breeches. He dried himself off as best he could before he began dressing in the new, dry clothes. He had denim pants that had a tag on the back that read "Levi Strauss and Co." He pulled them on, followed by the flannel shirt. He had no choice but to put his wet leather boots back on; no footwear was found with the new clothes.

A cold breeze blew through the tunnel, so he donned his new winter coat. The coat was a long one that had fur around the opening of the hood. He picked up the torch and began walking.

The air grew colder and the wind stronger as he neared the end of the tunnel; snowflakes swirled at his feet. He zipped his coat higher and pulled on the strings to tighten the hood. The end of the tunnel was white, and as he neared it he saw the snow flying horizontally. There was a snowdrift forming on the floor of the tunnel when he reached the end. He stood in the opening and looked out. He could see silhouettes of nearby trees, the rest was just a blanket of white. He stepped out of the stone tunnel and the wind nearly knocked him over. The snow poked at his face like the tips of toothpicks. He decided to take shelter back in the tunnel and wait out the storm, but when he turned around the archway opening to the tunnel was gone.

He walked forward with no idea what direction he was heading or what lay ahead. There were knee-high snowdrifts in some spots, and in others the ground was blown bare of snow. A concrete walk appeared and disappeared in and out of the drifts.

He walked by a few trees and saw a building; after he crossed the street he noticed a "closed" sign hanging on the door. He saw a street sign that said "Porter St." and he kept walking. For two blocks he walked, leaning his head sideways into the wind; all the businesses he passed were closed. He reached a cross street named "Trumbull" and noticed a parking lot across the way; a building stood in the middle of the lot. Cars filled a few of the parking spots. A sign in front of the building read "The Corktown Inn." He went to the front doors of the building and found them unlocked. He walked in as snow swirled around him and into the building; the door shut behind him as he let his eyes adjust from the blinding white of the storm.

A man sat at the lobby desk, strumming an out-of-tune acoustic guitar. The lobby was dim. A television sat on the counter next to the man; the screen of the television was blank. The man nodded as Raistlin approached.

"Hello," Raistlin said.

The man nodded again.

"Is there a room available?" Raistlin asked.

The man set the guitar on a chair next to him, "One night?"

"Yes," Raistlin said. A quick shiver went up his spine from the cold outside, his wet boots, and his wet hair.

The man turned to a pegboard full of keys, pulled one down, and dropped it to the counter. "It's 26 for one night. The power is out 'cause of the storm, but you can get to your room."

Raistlin stood and realized he had no way to pay. He felt his pants pockets, front and back, all empty. He reached into his coat pockets, they were empty as well. He felt inside his coat and noticed an inside pocket; he reached in and pulled out a leather wallet. He opened it, there were small pockets that held a few cards; The big pocket in the wallet held cash. Raistlin pulled out thirty dollars and slid them to the man. "Can I get one of those papers as well?"

"You from around here?" The man asked as he got him his change and handed him a newspaper.

Raistlin shook his head.

The man nodded, "Never would have guessed," he said and handed Raistlin his change. "There will be coffee here in the lobby in the morning. A pop and candy machine is by the ice machine down the hall, but the ice machine is broken. Actually, none of it will work until the juice is back on. Everything is closed today because of the storm, but there is a deli two blocks away; maybe they'll open tomorrow when they clean the streets." The man pointed to a hallway, "You're in room 23, just that way down the hall."

Raistlin nodded and thanked the man, then found his way to his room.

The room was dark. Raistlin stumbled his way to the window and opened the heavy curtains. Enough daylight made it through the blowing snow to light up the room, showing dust in the air from opening the curtains. Raistlin hung his coat on the only chair in the room and removed his wet boots. A small dresser stood in front of a mirror; the desk had a television sitting on top. The only other things in the room were a bed and a few pictures hanging on the walls.

He walked toward the bathroom and flipped a switch by the door. "Power is out," Raistlin whispered to himself, "He told me that."

He reached into the shower and found that the water was still working. He messed with the knobs until the water was warm. He stripped down and stood in the shower until the water cooled. He dried himself and walked back to the window with a bath towel wrapped around his waist and another wrapped around his shoulders to fend off the chill in the unheated room. The snow outside continued to blow, the howl of the wind was the only noise he could hear; there was no traffic or people in the streets. He reached into the coat that hung on the chair and pulled the wallet out. He pulled one card out; it was a plastic card with 16 numbers on it. On the bottom corner of the card the name "Mason Barrow" sat in raised white letters. He pulled out the other card, at the top it read "Michigan Driver License." It had a picture of him on the front, although he had never had his picture taken in his life. There was other information on the card, like his height and weight. Next to DOB, it read 7-16-1947. That date meant nothing to him in the world he came from.

He set the wallet on the dresser and picked up the newspaper. Above the front headline, it read, "January 14, 1992".

24

Sometime during the night, Raistlin woke to a sound inside the room. It was the heater kicking on, and the light in the bathroom was on. Raistlin crawled out of bed and flipped the light switch off, then hurried back to bed under the warm covers.

When he woke again, the room was warm and sunlight shined through the open curtains. The snow had stopped. He walked to the window and saw machines and plows moving snow from the streets.

Later that day he walked to a fuel station on Michigan Avenue. He purchased some snacks, a few toiletries, a six pack of beer, and a map. There was a rack of used books near the counter. He fished through the rack and found a book by a man named Steinbeck called *Pastures of Heaven*. The title reminded him of home, so he bought the book. Before he set his stuff on the counter, he spotted a composition journal. He snagged that and paid for his things.

On his way back to the hotel he stopped at the deli and bought a ham and pastrami sandwich and a Reuben sandwich. When he walked out of the deli, he realized that the empty lot across the street was where he came out of the tunnel. He walked through the empty lot with no sign of a stone archway. When he got back to the hotel, he paid for two more nights before he went to his room.

That evening, he opened a can of beer that had "Labatt Blue" written on the side. He pulled one of the sandwiches from his coat pocket and took a bite. Then he pulled the journal out and opened it to the first page. He found a pen on the dresser with the name of the hotel inscribed on the side. He began to write:

January 15, 1992

The weather here can be unbearable! Yesterday when I arrived the wind whipped the snow so hard it felt like getting poked in the face with dozens of sewing needles at once. And I have never seen so much snow in one place or felt this wicked, cold air. After the storm passed, big machines moved the snow off the streets and had it hauled away. To where? I don't know.

I paid for a map at a fuel station this morning, so I know where I am. Not that it matters. I go back to where the stone arch stood, but it is not there. At some point, it should appear, and Dorn will walk through and find me— but only if The Great Fathers have figured out a plan.

Raistlin J. Barrow

Pawns of the In Between

Part III: New Arrival

The arrival of Jake and Nana and the last two dragons brought a friendly roar from Donte. Brutus circled around with Jake and Nana holding reins that were tied around his neck. Alonzo followed obediently behind with a small amount of cargo strapped to his back. Donte's roar emptied Raistlin's cabin as Tessa, Cambria, and Anastasia came out into the late afternoon sun. When Alonzo landed after Brutus, he immediately started squirming around to try to get the cargo from his back. Hawley, who had been tending to the dragons since Dorn left, came running up from the barn when he saw the dragons land.

Hawley operated the lumber mill that was owned by Raistlin and Dorn, and he was an old friend of the family. He was a lanky man with short gray hair and always wore a cowboy hat, except while eating. He moved around the two dragons as if he were a man younger than his years. He calmed Alonzo, then helped Nana climb down from Brutus.

"Ma'am," Hawley said with his gruff voice.

"Hello, Hawley," Nana said.

Jake slid down from the dragon, "Hawley," he said and shook his hand. "It's been years."

"It sure has, Jake," Hawley said as he held Alonzo's reins.

"Grandpa! Nana!" Anastasia sprinted up and threw her arms around Jake's waist.

Jake picked her up, "Hello, Baby Doll," and smothered her with kisses.

Cambria walked up next with her swollen belly. Nana took Cambria's hands and held them out. "We came as soon as we got the message from the dove," Nana said. "You are getting close."

Cambria gave a wide smile and hugged Nana.

"Hello, Tessa," Jake said as Tessa approached. "Where is everyone else?"

"They had to leave," Tessa said as she hugged him.

Jake nodded without a word.

The ladies walked back to the house as the men removed the cargo from the dragon.

. . .

Sally returned from town at dusk, rode Goldie down to the barn, watered and fed her, and then walked back up to the houses. Jake was starting a campfire in the fire pit.

"I see that boy finally came to his senses and married you," Jake said as Sally approached.

"Yeah, it took him a while," Sally said and gave Jake a hug.

"Congratulations," Nana leaned forward in her chair and held out her hand for Sally to shake. "You'll be miserable for the rest of your life."

"I heard that," Jake said as he struck the flint a few times.

"At least you won mayor, though," Nana ignored Jake. "That will be fun for a bit."

Once the fire was blazing, Jake sat down and poured a glass of whiskey from a bottle. He looked at Tessa, "How long have they been gone?"

"Several weeks now."

"Who went?" Jake asked.

"Dorn, Jared, and Billy," Tessa said.

"Billy?" Jake lowered his glass before he took a sip.

Cambria nodded with a smile, "Billy came back."

Jake smiled and leaned back in his chair.

26

Sally spent less time at the saloon now that she was mayor of Ironwood. There were two other hostesses who managed the everyday duties for her. Her personal property was leased out to the new blacksmith in town since the death of Abraham Polk.

Her first duty as mayor was to renovate an empty building downtown and make it a doctor's office. With this improvement, Dr. Jones could help people in his own office as opposed to going to a family's home in a buggy pulled by his horse. To accomplish this, Sally would have to raise taxes one way or another. She thought about putting a tax on alcohol from her own saloon. Those drunks tossed money around like it was scrap paper that they didn't want in their pockets anymore. They would hardly notice the increase.

Another order of business was to strengthen the Sheriff's Office. Creed Thompson was getting up in age. He could handle his duties, and when something came up that he couldn't handle, there was usually a helping hand to take care of the dirty work. The townspeople respected him too much to give him much trouble. If anyone was arrested, Creed usually had a cup of coffee with that person through the jail bars until the person cooled their jets.

So, the threat wasn't within Ironwood, it was from across the river in Greystone, Lance and his cronies. Sally wasn't sure what had happened that night at the castle, except Jared was nearly killed and Raistlin disappeared. She knew Dorn went through something difficult that night, but she couldn't get him to talk about it. They would lay in bed at night, the moonlight shining through the window reflecting off Dorn's chest. She attempted to ask him a few times, but he would just put his arm around her and say nothing in response.

If a threat came, it would be out of Creed Thompson's hands. She needed someone tough, quick thinking, and quick on their feet to fill the office. She had someone in mind: a horse trainer who lived on the west side of town, down by the river. She might be just the right person.

The town needed a few more buildings and more opportunities for entrepreneurs to come in and stake out their businesses. More businesses in town meant more tax dollars and less strain on the local community. Sally's tough reputation as a bar owner made her unafraid of any reaction from the people. She was voted in for a reason, and it was time for the town to improve. She was a well-respected woman and won the vote by a landslide. Whatever calls she made, she was confident there would be little flack.

Marrying Dorn was quite the change for Sally. She had been a single woman for a long time, never dating anybody. She had a crush on Dorn for years, and she knew he had the same for her. There were times they would go on evening horse rides, or he would come to her house when her dog had pups. Always leaving with a gentlemanly kiss on the cheek. Then when he came back from the fight at the castle, something in him had changed. They fell fast in love, just as she had always hoped.

27

"Sally!" Then there was banging at the door. "Sally! It's time!"

It was Anastasia's voice. Sally sprang out of bed; it was still dark. She slipped into her robe and headed out of the bedroom to the front door. She opened it, and Anastasia stumbled in, "Sally! My sister's having the baby!"

"Okay, Sweetie! Wait here," Sally walked back into the bedroom. A minute later, she came out wearing pants, a cotton shirt, and a leather vest, and she was pulling her hair back into a ponytail. "Let's go," she said and followed Anastasia out the door. Lulu lay on her blanket in the kitchen and watched them leave.

Jake was heading out the door of Raistlin's cabin when Sally and Anastasia approached. "I have a fire started, Sally. That water needs boiling. Anastasia! Come with me!" Jake said.

When the water was nearly boiling, Jake and Anastasia came back with three more pails of water, then they left to get more firewood from the woodpile.

Sally poked her head in the bedroom, "Need anything?"

Nana sat beside the bed with her hand on Cambria's stomach. Tessa stood off to the side at the edge of the oil lamplight. "I think we are okay," she said.

Cambria let out a scream and arched her back.

"Easy," Nana said. "Deep breaths."

"The water is boiling. Holler when you need something," Sally said and ducked out of the room.

Jake and Anastasia returned with more firewood. As Jake was throwing logs into the woodstove, Cambria screamed again. Nana's voice was heard, but the words were indecipherable. A moment later, Tessa came out of the bedroom.

"The baby is breech!" She said.

Sally headed to the door. "I'll get the doctor," she said.

Sally sprinted down to the barn, her brown ponytail bouncing on her back as she ran. She slid the door open and grabbed her saddle. She tossed it on Goldie, strapped it down, and hopped on the horse. With a quick jab of the heels into the horse's sides, they were racing down the road to Ironwood. Sally held tight to the reins and cheered the horse on as they raced down the moonlit road. Minutes later, they reached the doctor's house.

"Dr. Jones!" She yelled and pulled the horse to a stop. She yanked on the leather reins, and the horse rose, standing on its hind legs. It let out a squeal, adding to the urgency of the situation. Sally slipped off the horse and was at the front door of the house when the doctor opened it.

"Barrow Homestead!" Sally said, "The baby is breech!"

The doctor stood in the doorway, his gray hair pointed in odd directions. "Get my horse, hook him to the buggy. I'll be right out." Then he slammed the door.

While Sally was hooking up the buggy to the horse, the doctor came out with his medicine bag in hand. He hopped into the seat on the buggy as Sally ran back to Goldie. She kicked her horse up to speed and the doc followed, his buggy bouncing down the road.

Sally burst into the cabin and the doctor followed her through the door. He nodded at Jake and said, "Where?"

Jake pointed to the closest doorway. The doctor walked through the door; Anastasia sat on her feet on a wicker loveseat in the hall.

After loud screams from Cambria, pacing on the floor from Jake, and anxious leg shaking from Anastasia, they finally heard a baby cry. Sally put her hands to her mouth and tears welled in her eyes. Anastasia was frozen on the loveseat, her mouth open. Jake stopped pacing, closed his eyes, and tilted his face to the ceiling.

Minutes later, Tessa walked out of the bedroom with the baby in her arms. "I am a grandmother," she said.

Jake walked to her and pulled the blanket to see the baby's face. "Another miracle," he said.

Anastasia sat at attention on the couch. Tessa came over and sat next to her, then carefully handed her the baby. Anastasia held the bundle like it was two dozen eggs piled on one another; one move and it would be ruined.

The doctor came out of the bedroom next, looking down at his bag as he buttoned it.

Jake stood, "Great work, Doc."

The doctor nodded and put out his hand, "How have you been, Jake?"

"I couldn't be better," he said as he took his hand.

Sally wiped her tears and said, "It's almost dawn, let me put coffee on." She poured water into a kettle and put it on the stovetop.

Nana came out of the bedroom. Jake looked at her and said, "Well?"

"She's asleep."

Nana sat down on a chair next to Jake; he took her hand. She pulled their hands to her chest and smiled at him. She was a tough woman, and always showed toughness in front of others. But that moment showed true love that had endured decades, and there was nothing that was going to take it away.

28

Sally trotted Goldie down the lane. Trees lined each side of the stone path. The path dropped and then opened into a grass pasture. Down by the river was a log cabin where two children were taking turns hitting a rug hanging from a line, knocking the dust out. When they saw Sally, they both waved.

"Hi, Sally," they said in unison.

Sally smiled and waved, "Hi, kiddies!"

Just upriver from the cabin, Preston Thorton cast a line into the river, his stump of a wrist hung at his side. A few years before, Preston took a job at the lumber mill. His klutziness got the best of him on the third day of the job. While running a log through the blade to cut planks, he got his hand caught between the log and the rollers, as the log moved forward his hand came in contact with the big sawblade. That was the day Preston lost his left hand.

Many miracles happened after the accident. One was that he didn't bleed to death. Another was his recovery from an infection that took hold of him after the wound was buttoned up.

On the other side of the cabin, Emily Thorton worked her horse in a large running pen. Sally redirected Goldie and went to see Emily.

Emily saw Sally approaching, pulled the bridle from her horse, and left the animal in the pen. She leaned against the gate while Sally rode up.

"Well, hello there Mrs. Mayor," Emily said. Her blonde hair was in a braid that was pulled over her shoulder, draping over her stout upper body. "What brings you out to the river?"

"I just thought I'd stop in and say hello," Sally smiled.

Emily smiled back, "Naw, you didn't. I know you enough, Sally. What's on your mind?"

Sally gazed off into the distance for a moment. She looked at the kids, then out at the husband. Preston was pulling a trout off the hook. Sally swung her leg over the horse and dismounted. She took the reins and tied the horse to the fence.

"I have a proposition for you," she said after she turned to face Emily.

"More saloon work?" Emily asked. She had worked at the saloon for some time, but when her husband lost his hand she had to spend all of her time at home while he recovered. The family had lived off farming, hunting, trading, and training horses ever since.

"Not exactly," Sally said. "I need help on the town level."

Emily tilted her head slightly, "What kind of help y'all need?"

"I'm putting Creed in a clerical role, at least until he agrees to retire." Sally bit her bottom lip for a second. "I'm looking for a new sheriff. I plan to appoint someone."

Emily looked toward the river at her husband. "I don't know, he's pretty limited with one hand."

"I mean you," Sally looked at Emily with stern eyes.

"Me? Why?"

"You have stature and grit. You can defend yourself well; everyone knows that. You won't be taken advantage of. Creed worries me. He's been a good man to the town, but it's time to move forward. There may be some business additions in the future; more people in town." Sally looked back out toward the river. "I think Preston can handle the kids, no?"

Emily gazed toward her husband, "He can handle it. We've just been doing our thing since the accident." She turned to Sally, "Let me talk to him; I'll let y'all know."

"Okay," Sally said as she untied the leather reins from the fence. "Your children are getting so big," she said as she watched the siblings pull the rug down from the line.

"I know, it seems like they were born just yesterday. Time just sneaks away."

"It does, doesn't it," Sally said then climbed onto her horse. "Think it over, Emily. I'll be in touch." Sally turned the horse and trotted back up the lane.

"Ah, heck," Emily hollered. "I been fixin' to do somethin' anyway. When do I start?"

29

Sally and Emily made their rounds about town. They approached every member of town with two pieces of news. One was that Emily was the new sheriff in town, and the other was that Creed Thompson would be coming around to collect a seasonal tax. Sally explained the tax and how it would be used for town improvements, and any local entrepreneur would have a great opportunity to build a business in Ironwood. Like Sally thought, most of the town didn't show much fuss. Some got a sad look in their eyes when she broke the news, but when she told them there would be a doctor's office in the middle of town, their mood brightened a bit.

Emily didn't don a sword like Creed always did, she only had a dagger with a six-inch blade tucked away in her leather vest. She knew she would never have to pull it on any townsfolk, the evil across the river was the reason she carried it. The citizens of Greystone were forbidden to cross the river. Not forbidden by anyone in Ironwood, but by Lance Erikson. Most of the people in Ironwood knew about the tension between Erikson's lot and the folks surrounding Dorn. They heard the story, which was becoming folklore, about the brutal killing of Dominic Hale so many years ago. An appalling death; something unheard of in Evergreen until the murder of Abraham Polk. Many knew that this feud between families was brewing, and they knew it could turn into a battle. Some had already been recruited, voluntarily, to be ready to fight. The Barrows and the Hales were the kindest, most generous families in all of Evergreen; most would do anything for them and expect nothing in return.

. . .

Back at the homestead, Cambria was back at her usual chores. She labored around the gardens with the baby strapped in a leather carrying pouch that hung around her shoulders. The pouch had been made by Raistlin when Anastasia was born.

Jake had taken two of the dragons back to the cabin to tend to the crops and the animals, Nana stayed back to help around the homestead. Cambria had spent so many years with Nana that she would have felt a little odd without her. When Cambria grew tired, she passed the baby off to Nana, who would rock him on the back deck and sing lullabies to him. The baby grew by the day, his nutrition coming from his mother's milk. Sally was in and out, taking care of the duties of a mayor of a small town; she longed for Dorn to return. Anastasia kept quiet, a little overwhelmed by all the attention to the baby, and she missed Billy.

Part IV: Dee-troit, Michigan

They sat across from each other in the dimly lit bar; sconces gave off a little glow against the dark wooden walls. The solid oak table separated them. On the table sat plates with half-eaten burgers and a handful of fries. One glass with amber-colored beer was only a quarter full; the other glass had a light-colored beer that was half full. Back at the entrance to the bar stood a carved mannequin dressed as a Red Coat soldier. The place was packed, and had they not made a reservation, they would still be waiting at the entrance while standing next to the wooden soldier.

"My Uncle Joe makes the best burger," Josh said as he held the burger in his hand. "I think this one would give him a run for his money. I hate to say it, but this may be better than his. I'll never tell him though." Then Josh took another big bite, the house sauce dripped onto his plate. His hair fell just above his eyes in big curls, in the back it was cut short.

"I know. The first time I came here I was amazed. We ate at home almost always while I grew up, we didn't go out much." Samira took a sip of her beer, pulled locks of her dark hair behind her ear, and took another bite of her burger.

"You gonna be able to eat all that?" Josh smiled at her, showing an attractive set of chompers.

"Pshh, I'll probably have to finish yours for you," she looked at him with her dark eyes.

Josh laughed, "I'll have to finish your burger *and* your beer."

"Not a chance," she said, and they both laughed.

They met at a concert eight months earlier in Ferndale at a place called The Loving Touch. He rode with two of his friends from college to see the concert. She came alone, leaving her homework at her apartment to finish the next day. She couldn't pass up a chance to see Real Estate, one of her favorite bands. They bumped into each other as he was walking away from the bar, trying to hold three beers and keep them from spilling over the top. She was heading to the bar with an empty glass.

"Oh," Josh said as he balanced the beers, not losing a drop.

"Oh my gosh, I'm sorry," she said.

"All good," he said, and smiled at her.

When she got another beer and turned away from the bar, he stood before her, smiling at her. "Wow," she jokingly said. "Did you drink those other two beers already?"

He laughed, showing a beautiful smile. "No, those were for my friends." He looked around for a moment. "We are close to the stage. You want to hang with us?"

"Of course," she said; her beautiful eyes swept him off his feet.

They watched the concert, and only a small group of people separated them from the stage. They talked in between songs. When the show was over, they took a selfie, the two of them standing together with the entire band stooping down on the stage to fit in the picture. After the show they stood outside the bar, Josh's friends blew clouds from their vapes into the night air and shivered as Josh and Samira chatted and giggled.

He was a student at Michigan State University, much to the chagrin of his parents, studying vet medicine. She was studying to be a dentist at a school in downtown Detroit.

They exchanged numbers when they parted ways that night, and the moment Josh was settled in his dorm in Lansing, he called Samira. She answered immediately, and they talked until the sun was peeking through their windows.

Even though they were over an hour apart, they always found a way to see each other. Usually, he drove his mid-size pickup to Detroit on the weekends; from there they would check out the Motown Hall of Fame, or see a jazz band in the area, and they were both excited for baseball to start in the spring. At first, he crashed on her couch when he stayed, soon they would wake together in the same bed.

31

Josh went home for the three weeks in between the spring and summer semesters to help on the farm. Being a farmer was a never-ending job; even after the crops were planted there were things to fix and maintain, and the animals always needed to be tended to. Uncle Joe had grown his cattle numbers. When Josh was a kid, there were only two or three cows, now the numbers were twelve to fifteen. Along with farming hundreds of acres, Uncle Joe and Josh's father each had an enormous garden. Josh's mom and Uncle Joe's wife, Becky, went to the farmer's market every weekend in the summer and sold chicken eggs, tomatoes, carrots, bell peppers, banana peppers, cucumbers, and zucchini. Sometimes trades were made; two dozen farm fresh eggs for a pound of bacon.

Uncle Joe met Becky at Jared's funeral. Her son had been in basic training with Jared. She was from Fort Wayne, Indiana. At the wake after the funeral, they met and started chatting. Soon a long-distance relationship became a short one; she moved in with Uncle Joe, and soon they were married in a private ceremony. Two years later, to their surprise, she became pregnant; nine months later, Joseph Jared Collins was born. Everyone called him JJ.

Having Becky around may have saved Laura Collins's life. The death of her son put her in a deep depression for months. Once Becky came around, things lightened up for Laura a bit. It took time, but they became great friends. Becky pulled Laura out of her depression; she took her out to lunch, kept her busy in the garden, and treated her like a true friend.

Over the three-week break, Samira stopped down often, sometimes for several days. Uncle Joe, Aunt Becky, JJ, and Josh's parents all loved Josh's girlfriend. The evening that sealed the deal was when Samira showed up with grocery bags of ingredients from a market in Dearborn. She made a meal of couscous with roasted meats and fish.

During the week before they were to return to college, Josh took Samira on a three-day trip to Hocking Hills. When they started school again, their love was stronger than ever, as if it were chiseled in stone.

32

The heat of summer didn't keep the lovebirds from the ballpark. They tried to catch a game during every home stand.

Beers were aplenty on this muggy Saturday afternoon at the ballpark. Josh and Samira stuck with bottled water, but during the sixth inning, they grabbed an ice cream. She sat in jean shorts that showed off her legs. Her top was a loose tank top that slipped off her shoulder often, showing the strap from a bathing suit top. Her dark hair was pulled into a ponytail, which added an accent to her strong cheekbones and beautiful, dark eyes. He wore dark blue shorts and a pair of Hey Dudes; his shirt was a button-up white linen short-sleeve. He wore aviator sunglasses, just like his brother always did. Although Josh had some awkward teen years in the looks department, he was now a handsome young man. He had many features like his brother; a beautiful smile and chiseled face attracted the attention of any young woman who walked by. He was lankier than his brother, but still carried a toned frame, and the curly hair that fell into his eyes was much different than his brother's typical military cut.

"My friends that live in the duplex are watching their neighbor's dog, and I told them I would help out. Just letting him out and feeding him," Samira said, then she took a bite of chocolate ice cream.

"Is the dog staying with them?"

"No," she said as she wiped the corner of her mouth with her finger. "They don't want to keep him at their place. If the landlord found out they had a pet the rent would go up, so they just go over there a bunch."

"Is the guy on vacation or something?" Jared asked.

"No," she paused, watching the game. "He is in a nursing home. He told them it wouldn't be long, but we are all skeptical. He's pretty old. Nicest guy in the world, I've met him twice; just a wonderful person."

"What breed of dog?" Josh asked as he scraped the bottom of his ice cream cup.

"I'm not sure, what's that one dog? Airedale? Sweet dog, he seems bummed that his owner is gone, though."

"It's crazy how much focus we, as humans, can put on the feelings of the animals that we love. We sometimes forget about the people around us, their feelings, and their mental health; but we will be worried about a lonely dog, or a cat that has to live out in a barn, which is probably a dream for most felines. Yet, most people want to walk away the week after the funeral of a friend with hopes the family can handle it without more help. Although, on the same token, those animals that we are so worried about will show an unconditional love that is unmatched by most people. A love that has no boundaries." Josh put the empty ice cream cup in the cupholder next to him. "A love that doesn't care about race or politics. 'Feed me, scratch my ears, take me for walks, and I will do anything for you.' It's a wonderful thing, really, and a shame that our furry four-legged friends are the only ones that collectively hold that trait."

The entire time he spoke, she gleamed at him with dreamy eyes. When he finished talking, she said, "Well, well, the wisdom of the future Dr. Collins."

. . .

They went to Samira's friend's duplex to check on Atticus.

"Why did he name him Atticus?" Josh asked as they walked away from his truck and down the sidewalk toward the duplex.

Samira turned up a sidewalk to a duplex and then walked into the flower bed. She lifted a small rock and took a key off the ground. "He said to the dog, 'I'm going to take you back to the shop, maybe someone will come looking for you. I'll call you Atticus." She slipped the key into the lock and said, "He's had him ever since."

"Sounds like a win-win situation," Josh said.

A loud, deep bark sounded when she opened the door.

"Atticus, it's me," she said and walked through the door.

The dog lightened up and greeted Samira, but did a soft growl when he saw Josh.

Josh knelt, held his hands out below his hips, and said, "Hey buddy!" in a higher pitched voice than his usual mid-range. Atticus was cautious at first, but then spent twenty or thirty seconds giving Josh the sniff test. Then he was happy enough to nudge Josh's hand for a good petting, all the while covering his hand with slobber.

Atticus was a tall dog with somewhat small paws for his size. He had a tail that curled forward and touched his back. He was thin, but not thin enough to see his ribs. His small ears flipped forward and were always at attention. His snout was dense and long. His tan and brown fur was showing signs of white in the chest. His eyebrows were also showing a touch of white along with his long wiry beard. The dog's brown eyes always seemed to be studying the scenario at hand.

Samira walked out of the kitchen with a dog leash in her hand, "Okay, Atticus." She clicked the leash to the dog's collar and the three of them walked outside.

"I'm just going to feed him, then we can go," she said when they walked back in.

"That's fine, we're not in a hurry," Josh said. Atticus rolled on the carpet onto his back, wiggling back and forth and groaning. Josh smiled and sat on the couch. He picked up a picture frame on the end table next to him. Atticus was in the picture; his owner had his arm draped around the dog. The man's face was slightly turned away from the camera, laughing; the dog was trying to lick the man's face, and the picture looked like an attempted selfie. Josh put the picture frame back on the table. The end table was the type with a wide base and a shelf below. All the furniture in the room was aged and unmatched. The dwelling was clean, but most of the stuff was second-hand; as a college student living away from home, this second-hand furniture was a comfort to Josh.

On the lower part of the table was a book; it had a black cover with nothing on it. Josh picked it up, wondering what it was. He pulled it open and saw handwriting on the first page. What he thought may have been a book with its dust jacket removed was a notebook or journal of some sort. The first page was half full of writing. He immediately closed the book, feeling like he had stepped over the bounds of someone's privacy. By the time Samira walked back into the room, the journal had been placed on the lower shelf of the end table.

"Ready?" she asked. "My friends will let him out later, it's all good."

"Sure," Josh stood up. "Let's go."

33

They made their way out of the park, walked through a small playground, and took a sidewalk along Atwater Street toward the GM towers. Billy led the way, and Jared kept glancing across the river toward Canada. Dorn was mesmerized by the tall buildings before him. Once they reached the base of the towers, Dorn walked off the sidewalk and into traffic to get closer to the buildings.

Jared grabbed Dorn's leather vest, "Whoa, buddy. This isn't Ironwood. These cars can kill you when they run you over."

"Yes," Dorn stumbled back onto the sidewalk. "Of course." He looked up at the tall structure before him, "Those buildings!"

Jared stood next to him and said, "Yeah, something, huh?"

"Are we on a sightseeing tour, or looking for Raistlin?" Billy said while walking backward to look at the two men.

"Sorry, Billy," Dorn said. "I didn't mean to hold you up. On with the mission!"

Jared glanced at Dorn and grinned.

They made their way past a parking garage and through a dusty parking lot, and then the sidewalks opened up to a large concrete area with a fountain in the center. People wandered the open area, some dressed in muggy weather attire, some dressed for business. Two food trucks sat across the sparse crowd of people. One was a taco truck, the other a barbeque truck.

Once they passed by the fountain, a little amphitheater spread out below them; three musicians belted out jazz sounds. A woman played on a small drum set, a tall man plucked a stand up bass, and a man with dreadlocks made his way through jazz scales on a hollow body guitar.

Billy kept walking as if everything was normal. Jared was filled with joy at the downtown staple that was before him. Dorn was glued on the musicians, stopping every few steps to watch.

They made their way back to the sidewalk, then they took a right on Washington Blvd. They walked between buildings that only Billy knew; Dorn continued to gape at the structures that towered over him.

They crossed over the freeway while they walked down Howard Street; soon they were on Porter Street. They walked to a sign that read, "Murphy Playlot."

Jared stopped walking, and Dorn stopped when Jared stopped.

"Billy," Jared said.

Billy stopped walking and looked back.

"I remember this," Jared said. "Me and Josh stopped here. I parked my truck right over there," he pointed.

Billy nodded and pointed to the next street, "I grew up just around the corner."

They took a right on Brooklyn Street, then another right on Labrosse Street. They walked two houses down to a vacant lot.

"This is where I grew up," Billy pointed to a vacant lot. "My house was here as a kid," he said. "But long after I grew up and Mom sold the house, it burned to the ground. The man's wife was killed by a nutcase at her work, and he..."

"... drank himself to oblivion, and passed out smoking a cigarette in the middle of the night," Jared finished the sentence for Billy.

"The house burned to the ground," Billy and Jared said in unison.

Billy looked at Jared with a surprised look. Jared gave him a respectful nod.

They stood for a few moments; Billy had his hands stuffed in his pockets, he stood in the same spot he did so many years ago playing round-up, tag, or war.

After a few moments, Jared spoke up, "You guys hungry?"

Dorn looked down at the ground and nodded.

Billy finally pulled himself away from the vacant lot and said, "Sounds good."

They walked back down Labrosse Street and took a left on Brooklyn. When they reached Murphy Playlot they noticed a deli across the street.

"Let's grab a bite," Jared said as he looked at the sign above the deli that read "Mudgie's Deli & Wine Shop."

"Sounds good," Dorn said as they crossed the street.

The deli was a little shop on the corner. There was construction going on one side of the shop, which Jared later learned was from a recent fire. They stood before the counter and contemplated the menu.

Billy spoke first, "I know what I want. I want the Leggo my Daggo."

Jared nodded to the girl behind the counter, "Put that down for him. I'll take the Brooklyn."

"Okay," the girl said. "The Leggo my Daggo for the little guy, the Brooklyn for you." She looked at Dorn, "And what about you, sir?"

"I'll have the Press-Lee."

"The Pressley, sure," the girl punched the order into a computer. "Drinks?"

"How about Cokes for each of us," Jared said as he pulled out his wallet.

"Are you an Elvis Pressley fan?" Billy asked Dorn.

Dorn gave him a blank look, "Who's Elvis Pressley?"

Billy cocked his head to the side for a moment, "Hmmm… Yeah, I guess you wouldn't know him."

While they waited for their food, Dorn studied the signs on the wall.

When they received their food, they decided to take it outside and eat at a picnic table at the park.

Once the first bites were taken, the conversation disappeared. Although the food in Evergreen was always a good home cooked meal, these sandwiches were a step into Jared and Billy's world. Neither Jared nor Billy had experienced a sandwich with melted cheese and other toppings in quite some time, and Swiss cheese and rye bread were things Dorn had never experienced before.

Billy lay on the picnic table bench with a quarter of his meal still sitting on the table; he groaned and complained of eating too much. Dorn and Jared sipped on their sodas in silence, both amazed at the great meal.

"Is that a hotel up there?" Jared asked.

Billy sat up and looked, "Yeah, probably."

Jared looked up at the sky, "We should check it out, it won't stay light forever."

. . .

They checked into the Trumbull and Porter Hotel two blocks from Murphy Playlot. They let Billy work the key card that opened the door to their room. After he opened it, he immediately dropped his backpack and ran for the first of two queen beds in the room. Just before he reached the bed, he leapt into the air and yelled, "Belly smacker!" After he landed on the bed, he was bounced off toward the other bed. He yelled, "Whoa!" as he flipped feet first in the air and crashed to the ground.

"Jeepers," he said as he used the edge of the bed to pull himself back to his feet.

The other two laughed.

. . .

Jared looked out the hotel window at the Motown lights. Dorn slept on the first bed in the room, and Jared's rustled sheets lay on the second bed as Billy slept curled up in the recliner. Jared lost himself in thought as he gazed into the night.

Earlier in the day he learned that the year was 2022. It had been several months since he had seen his family, but a decade since they had seen him. At first, it boggled his mind, but he understood the ways of the different worlds. Time was a peculiar thing. He wondered about his little brother, out there somewhere. Probably not in this city, but somewhere. He worried about his parents. He closed his eyes and prayed to God, and The Great Fathers, that his parents were healthy and well. He longed to see them, to hug them, to apologize to them; apologize for breaking their hearts. How was he to know he would get killed in a war; he knew what was at stake when he enlisted, but nobody ever thinks it will happen to them. But, it was all worth it; he wouldn't change a thing. His country was worth it. He knew his family would heal if they hadn't already. He still wanted to hug all of them. He wanted to hug his father and tell him none of it was his fault. Their tumultuous relationship during Jared's teen years led to months of silence. When he left for boot camp, they shook hands, but both of them were too stubborn to grab the other in a bear hug. And, Lord, how he missed his mother; if he could just see her once more.

When Jared crawled back into his bed, the night sky was beginning to glow in the east.

34

They went back to her apartment and showered off the stickiness of the day, then they headed off to Ferndale to check out another indie band. Before they went to The Loving Touch, the venue where they met, they went to Second Base, a comfortable little bar with good food. It was a staple of Ferndale.

They split a pepperoni pizza and a pitcher of beer, and they laughed and talked about dogs.

Samira reminisced about a pooch she had for a short while as a little girl. The dog's name was Tootsie, but after six months her parents told her it was too difficult to take care of it with their apartment living arrangements. In the end, it all worked out because Samira's cousin was able to take Tootsie, and Samira was able to visit the dog several times a month.

While Samira went on about the dog, Josh noticed a woman walking in their direction as he looked past Samira's shoulder. The woman was tall and blonde, she wore leather pants with high heels on her feet, and a thin white blouse. When Josh made eye contact with her, the woman stared him down. He held his gaze as their eyes locked. She looked at him as though she was trying to get his attention or seduce him. Although the woman was pretty, Josh had no interest in her. The only woman he had eyes for was the one sitting across from him eating pizza and talking about dogs. Nonetheless, Josh held his gaze on the tall blonde. He had never seen her before, but something was peculiar about her. As the woman came closer to the table, Josh kept staring at her.

"Hello?" Samira said. "Are you still with me?"

Josh didn't answer as he continued to lock eyes with the woman. When the woman walked by the table she touched Josh's left hand, ran her finger up his forearm, then continued to walk by.

"Whoa!" Samira said. "What was that?"

Josh glanced over his left shoulder as the woman walked away.

"Um, excuse me?" Samira sat up taller in her chair. "You want to tell me what that is all about?" Samira leaned to her right to see the woman better. "Who does she think she is?"

Josh put out his hand, "Wait!"

"Wait? What? What do you mean, wait?" Samira's voice was getting louder as she spoke.

Josh gently grabbed her hand and looked her in the eyes, "Please!" He glanced over his shoulder, then back at Samira, "Something's not right."

"You're damn right something's not right. You get googly-eyed over some girl approaching you, then she almost feels you up! Um, yeah!" Samira said as she crossed her arms and sank a little in her seat.

"No!" Josh snapped. "You don't get to say that. This isn't on me. Something strange just happened. Maybe the girl is just a psycho, I don't know. Can we just finish our pizza?"

They finished their meal and polished off the pitcher in silence. When they left, Josh stopped to use the restroom and Samira waited for him by the entrance of the bar. When he walked out of the restroom, Samira was talking with a man. The man had leather pants on, just like the woman from earlier in the evening. The man also wore a black T-shirt with the sleeves cut off. Tattoos riddled his arms; his black hair was pulled back in a ponytail that fell just past his shirt collar. Samira was pointing in one direction, then the other; she was giving him directions to somewhere.

As Josh approached, the man said, "Okay, thank you, dear." The man looked at Josh and nodded, then walked out the door.

Josh stopped in his tracks; the man was all too familiar, but Josh couldn't place who he was.

"Oh, what a nice guy," Samira said. "He was wondering how to get to I-75. Kind of odd for people to ask for directions nowadays."

Josh stood before her and didn't say a word; he was still trying to place who the man was.

"What's the matter?" Samira said. "Cat got your tongue? A man asks me for directions and now you're flabbergasted?"

It was then that Josh realized that the man who was asking his girlfriend for directions was Lance Erikson. Josh leaned forward and put his hands on his knees.

"Jeez, Josh. He only asked me for directions, not my number." Samira said as she stood by the door. "Can we go?"

Josh stood, "Sure."

. . .

Both Josh and Samira were quiet during the concert at The Loving Touch. A rift had developed from the events earlier in the night. After the show, they drove back to Samira's apartment in silence. They crawled into bed with the city lights leaving a glow in the room. Samira fell asleep quickly, but Josh lay on the bed and stared at the ceiling. After a million thoughts ran through his head, he fell asleep.

He woke as soon as the morning sun poked through the blinds. He tapped Samira, "Wake up."

"Umm," she groaned.

"I have to go home," Josh said.

She took a deep breath, "Why, neither of us has class until tomorrow."

"No, I mean home. Hickory."

She began to wake more. "To your parents?"

"Yes."

"Why?"

"I have to check something," He said as he stood up and grabbed his shorts. "I want you to go with me."

"Sure, Romeo," she scooted herself around to a sitting position against the headboard of the bed. "How many girls down there are going to hit on you?"

Josh turned and looked at her. "You need to go with me. This is important. Last night might make a little more sense once we talk more."

"Can I sleep for ten more minutes?"

"No, I'd like to go now."

. . .

When they left Detroit, Josh said, "I need you to listen to me. I want you to understand what I am about to tell you, just hear me out. Capisce?"

Samira sat in the passenger seat of his truck, "Yeah, sure."

Josh told her everything. How he found the door in his woods when he was twelve years old, to meeting Billy Blaine, to how Lance Erikson was an evil person that he thought he would never see again.

"There is so much more to tell you," Josh said as they drove by the sign along the highway that read "Welcome to Ohio." Suddenly, the road was much smoother. "I mean, if I wrote it all down, it would be a three hundred and seventy-page novel. But what I'm getting at, that guy last night at Second Base, the one that asked you for directions?"

Samira looked over at him, "What about him?"

"He is Lance Erikson, from Evergreen," Josh took his eyes off the highway to look at her. "He is here in our world, somehow."

Samira closed her eyes and shook her head, "Okay, this is crazy. When you told me the story about this magical world where you met these people, I kind of felt sorry for you." She turned in the seat to look at him again, his eyes were on the road. "You know those kids who have imaginary friends? Sometimes for years? I thought maybe that was your deal, that these people were all in your imagination as a kid. But now one of them is here? Pshh!" She sat back in her seat, "This is ridiculous! You should just turn around and take me back."

"It's all true, Sam," Josh said. "Every word of it."

"I," she sighed. "No. Just when you think you know someone."

"You do know me! I haven't changed."

"Why didn't I hear this story sooner? We've been dating for eight months!"

"Because you'd think I was nuts!"

"Damn right I do."

They sat at a red light at the top of the exit ramp, and Josh grabbed her hand, "Just trust me. Work with me on this. Something strange is happening here, and if it keeps happening, I don't think I can do it alone." He pulled her hand up and kissed it.

"Fine, prove to me you're not nuts," she said as he took a left at the light and headed into the countryside for the ten-minute drive to his family's farm.

35

Dorn messed with the coffee maker that sat on the dresser, "So, this thing makes coffee?"

Jared looked at him as he held his shirt in his hands, ready to pull it over his head, "Yes, but they might have coffee in the lobby. It'd be just as easy to get it there." A silver scar graced Jared's chest, a constant reminder of the fight at Erikson's Castle. He winced as he pulled the shirt over his head, the pain from the wound still lingered. "What should we do today, Dorn?"

"We should go back to that grassy area where we came out of the tunnel."

"The park?" Jared asked.

"Yes, the park," Dorn said. "We should check there first and see if the tunnel is back."

"If it's not?" Jared asked.

"Then we walk around until an idea strikes."

"You guys want a tour of Corktown?" Billy asked.

"Yes!" Jared said.

"A personal tour of Dee-troit from the one and only Billy Blaine," Dorn said.

Billy smiled as he fished a shirt out of his pack, his hair still wet from the shower.

"Jared," Dorn said. "We haven't checked that book."

"The Book of Secrets? No, we haven't." Jared nodded at Billy, "Hey, Billy, dig through my pack and get that book out."

Billy kneeled and shuffled through Jared's pack and found the book. He stood up and held it out as he walked it toward Jared.

"Go ahead, Billy, open it," Jared said.

Billy shrugged his shoulders and opened the book. He frowned for a moment, then flipped through more pages. He closed the book and held it up, "Nothing, all pages are blank."

"I figured as much," Jared said. "Let's head out. Billy, bring the book."

. . .

Jared and Dorn each carried a coffee and Billy carried a bottle of Coke as they neared Riverwalk Park. A breeze blew through the open area sending a little relief from the humid morning.

"I don't see the tunnel," Dorn said.

"Check the book, Billy," Jared said.

Billy opened the book, "Nothing."

"Okay," Jared said as he turned around and faced the city.

Billy tucked the book under his arm, "Ready for your tour?"

"Yes, we are, Mr. Blaine," Dorn said.

They headed back toward the hustle and bustle of the city. "Well, I'd show you the casinos, but they probably won't let me in, so let's go to Comerica."

"What's that?" Dorn asked.

"It's where the Tigers play," Billy said.

Dorn turned to Jared, "Is that the team of animals that – "

Jared cut him short, "No, it's people. They play a sport we call baseball."

Dorn nodded and gazed at the tall buildings as they walked.

A half an hour later they stood before Comerica Park. Dorn looked up at the stadium, "So, they play inside there?"

"Yep," Jared said. "Hey, let's go see if there is a game today." They walked around the stadium and found the ticket booth. After a few minutes, they walked away with three tickets for that evening's game.

"Jared," Billy looked up at him as they walked. "Did you ever see a game at Tiger Stadium?"

"Yep, I was young. It was even before Josh was born. I saw the last game there."

"I did too," Billy smiled. "September 27, 1999. The Tigers…"

"Beat the Royals 8 to 2," Jared chimed in to finish Billy's sentence.

"Wow," Billy said. "You are a true fan."

. . .

"Well, golly, would you look at that," Billy said as they stood on the corner of Michigan and Trumbull. Caddy-corner from where they stood a big sign read, "The Corner Ballpark." A sign to the left read, "Detroit Police Athletic League." From their perspective, a baseball diamond lay inside the structure, and bleachers stood just outside of the basepaths.

"They tore it down and built a ballpark anyway," Jared said in awe.

"How cool," Billy whispered.

"Do Tigers play here, too?" Dorn asked as he gazed at the beauty.

"No," Jared hesitated. "They used to have a stadium here, but it was torn down. I'm guessing the police and firemen have leagues, and maybe kids get to play here from time to time. Not sure though, this is the first I have seen it."

"There is nowhere as cool as Detroit, even though I have never been anywhere else," Billy said as he looked at The Corner Ballpark. "Well, except Evergreen." He turned to Jared and Dorn, "I have an idea, let's go get a pie!"

Jared and Dorn looked at each other, and Jared shrugged his shoulders.

"Shoot, I forgot, it's all the way past the Riverwalk," Billy said.

"What's the Riverwalk?" Dorn asked.

"That's where we walked out of the tunnel when we got here," Billy said.

Dorn nodded.

"Let's rent a car. I have a driver's license and a credit card," Jared said.

Billy raised his finger into the air and said, "Bingo bango."

Jared told the car rental company he didn't want anything smaller than a normal sized SUV or pickup truck. They set him up with a 2022 Chevy Tahoe. When they climbed in the vehicle all three of them were in awe.

"Woohoo, look at this baby!" Billy said as he climbed into the backseat.

"Wow," Jared said as he slid into the driver's seat.

Dorn stayed quiet as he looked around the vehicle after sitting in the passenger seat.

"Okay, where are we going, Billy?" Jared asked.

"Pizza Papalis, take a left here," Billy said. "We're probably ten minutes away."

. . .

The pieces of pizza were in a triangle shape and as thick as a stick of butter. They sliced into the meat, cheese, and sauce with the sides of their forks

102

as if they were eating an apple pie. A beer sat in front of each man and a root beer for Billy. The silence between the three as they ate was a tribute to how good the pizza pie tasted.

After the food and an uneventful baseball game, they sat in their hotel room.

"So, why are we here?" Jared asked Dorn while he sipped from a bottle of water.

"Let's hope the book will tell us," Dorn said and looked at Billy.

Billy grabbed the book and opened it, "Hey, look!" He held the book up to the others and quickly pulled it back in front of him, "It says, 'You are thirty years too late.'" The words were written in fine calligraphy in black ink.

Jared furrowed his brow, "Thirty years too late? That," then he jumped to his feet and yelled, "Billy!"

Billy screamed as the pages of the book caught fire in his hands. He dropped the book and jumped back. The book became entirely engulfed in flames, and by the time it hit the floor, it was a pile of ash. Billy's breathing was heavy as he looked at the remnants of the book.

"What the hell," Jared whispered. He looked over at Dorn who was sitting against the windowsill, sipping whiskey from a plastic cup.

Dorn shook his head, "Something isn't right. I've had a funny feeling since I met with The Great Fathers back in Evergreen."

"But, isn't your father a part of that group?" Jared asked.

"Yes, he is, but something is off. I'm not sure he realizes it, maybe it's just me." Dorn turned and looked out the window. "I just had a bad feeling when I sat in that cave."

"So, what now?" Jared asked.

"I don't know," Dorn said.

Jared grabbed one of the cups off the hotel ice tray, pulled the plastic wrap from it, and held it out to Dorn.

Dorn grabbed the bottle and poured him two fingers of bourbon.

36

Josh swiped his foot over the weeds; although still humid, the interior of the woods was much cooler than outside.

"This is where it was," he said.

"Where what was?" Samira looked at the ground.

"The door," he crossed his arms. "The door to the In Between."

"And that is where you met Billy? A kid that came straight from 1962?"

Josh looked at her and nodded.

"I don't believe in time travel," she pouted.

"I wouldn't either if all of that stuff hadn't happened to me," Josh held her hand and began walking toward his parents' house. "Billy came to Jared's grave a few months after the funeral, actually it would have been Jared's birthday that day. He showed me the scar, lifted his shirt, and showed me where the tree branch went through his side while we were in the Dark Forest. He was sixty-two years old when I saw him that day." Josh pushed a tree branch over his head for both to walk under. "If I wasn't convinced before that point, I was then. It was the last time I saw him."

They were both silent while they walked; when they cleared the woods Josh said, "I don't think they're home. Let's go in, I'll leave them a note."

After they entered the house, Josh said, "Come upstairs."

Josh went to his closet when they got to his room; he shuffled some things around and walked out of the closet with an old Nike shoebox. He walked to his bed and sat down; Samira sat in his old gaming chair and rolled to him. He sat the box on his lap and opened it, on top was an official looking envelope, and Josh set it aside. He pulled an arrowhead the color of slate out of the box. He turned it over in his hand for her to see, "Jared found this in the fields one day when I was young. He was so ecstatic, jumping up and down. But he gave it to me right away, he said it was an arrowhead from Tecumseh when he fought a war here."

"Tecumseh?" Samira asked. "I mean I've heard of the town in Michigan, but...?"

"Tecumseh was a Shawnee Indian warrior and a great man. I used to have a book called *Panther in the Sky*, it's fantastic. It tells all about his life. I'll look for it online, you'll love it." Jared put the arrowhead back in the box and pulled out a Purple Heart.

Samira let out a small gasp.

Josh looked at her and nodded, "I know, it's pretty special. Mom and Dad immediately gave me the medal when they received it from the Army. I slept with it under my pillow for a year." He set the medal back in the box and pulled out another envelope. He closed the lid and began pulling photos out of the envelope, setting the first few photos on top of the box. The first was Jared in his green fatigues; he was leaning against a pile of sandbags with an M16 across his lap.

The next pic was Jared and his squad. Josh pointed to Jared in the pic, "There's Jared. I've always felt that he said something at the right moment to get them all to smile."

The next photograph was of Josh, at twelve years old, and his brother as they stood in front of the old Chevy pickup truck. "Mom took this before we left on a hiking trip. It wound up being the trip of our lives."

The last picture he pulled out was of a young boy sitting on a log, eating food with his fingers out of a plastic container. "This is Billy. You know that old tree stand I pointed to earlier that is barely there anymore?" Josh looked up at Samira.

Samira nodded.

Josh pointed to a spot on the picture to the upper left of Billy's head, "There is that tree stand."

"How was he young here when you said the last time you saw him was when he was sixty-two?"

"This was the time he was stuck here. It's when I went to his house in 1962, and then he came here in 2012. The door disappeared after he got here. He had to stay for a few days before it reappeared."

"Did you get any pictures from the In Between or Evergreen?"

Josh shook his head, "No, I never thought of it. Once we got out of our world and I realized there was no cell phone service, I turned my phone off. I never thought about taking a picture. My phone sat at the bottom of my pack for months."

Josh gathered everything up and placed it back into the box, then he stood and walked to the closet, reached up, and set the box on a shelf.

When he sat back on the bed, Samira pulled his hands onto her lap, "You're about to think I am crazy."

"Crazier than me?" Josh smiled.

"Maybe not that crazy," she tucked a lock of hair behind her ear. "But, I believe you."

Josh took a deep breath. "All of it?"

"Yes, all of it. It all sounds crazy, like something you would read in a book. But, yes, I believe you."

He stood up, still holding her hands; she stood up with him. "Good," he said. "Because there is not another person on this planet that would believe this story." He gave her a quick kiss and a huge hug and lifted her off her feet. He set her back down and said, "Let's go back to Motown, I don't think we are going to find anything here."

37

Jared and Dorn watched the television with glassy eyes. A baseball game from the West Coast was playing with the volume down low enough that they could barely hear the game. Billy was crashed on the bed, his shoes still on his feet. Dorn sat in an office chair with his feet propped up on the desk, Jared was sprawled on the couch; both men held plastic cups in their hands that still held traces of bourbon.

"So, what do you think that book meant by 'thirty years too late?'" Jared asked. He spoke his words at a slow pace, careful not to jumble them together in his drunken state.

"Maybe Raistlin came and went thirty years ago," Although Dorn's eyes were glassy with booze, he spoke as if it was first thing in the morning after a cup of coffee.

"So, where is he now?" Jared asked as he gazed at the television.

"Only Raistlin and The Great Fathers know. Maybe he returned to Evergreen as soon as we left." Dorn took a sip from his cup.

"How will we find him?" Jared asked, his words slurred this time and his eyelids grew heavy.

"We just keep looking, something will come up. Or maybe we will be stuck here forever."

Jared's eyes popped open, and he looked over at Dorn. Just as he was about to speak, the volume on the television went up, and the game was interrupted in the middle of a double play with a commercial.

A man on the screen began talking in a heavy Scottish accent. He wore a red tunic that was held together with a leather belt. Behind him were tents and food trucks; people wandered the area with cups of beer in their hands.

"Aye, laddies and lassies," the man held his cup of beer in the air. "Come join us as we celebrate the Celtic Festival."

Dorn dropped his cup onto the floor, and a small splash of bourbon shot into the air.

"Come on down to St. Andrew's Hall for cold beer, great food, and reenactments from a time when the Celts ruled all of Europe."

Dorn scooted forward in his chair as the man continued. "That's," Dorn began.

Jared sat up on the couch while Dorn paused.

"That's Randall," Dorn whispered.

"Randall?" Jared asked.

"Randall Barrow," Dorn said. "That's Randall Barrow."

"Randall Barrow? Who is- Oh, wait! You mean?"

"Raistlin's grandfather! One of The Great Fathers! That is him as a young man." Dorn squinted his eyes at the television.

"Where in the hell did he get that accent?" Jared asked.

"He had a faint accent, nothing like this though. But that is him," Dorn said.

"What does this mean?" Jared asked.

"It means we are going to the Celtic Festival tomorrow."

38

Two men clacked wooden swords together in their tunics, their sandaled feet stirred up dust on the dry ground. The man in the gray tunic led an offensive that had the other man on his heels. They fought to cheers and jeers, the audience keeping a balance on their favorite fighter. The man in the black tunic began to gain ground, but then one of the swords broke in half.

"Not quite Star Wars, but still pretty cool," Josh said.

"Depends which Star Wars movie you are watching," Samira said.

"True, very true," Josh said, then took a sip from his bottle of water.

"What now?" Samira said as she looked around. The sun shined off her straight dark hair.

"Well, I think those food trucks are calling me," Josh said.

"I'm game," Samira said.

The row of food trucks sat perpendicular to the lane where Josh and Samira walked from the historic reenactment. When they reached the crossroads, a hot dog truck was the first one they saw. To follow true Celtic tradition, they were looking for a beef stew or a pork pie. As they walked by the hot dog truck a young boy said, "Aw, jeepers."

Josh stopped walking and held his hand out for Samira to stop. Josh turned and looked at the boy. The boy had dropped his half-eaten hot dog onto the ground.

Josh closed his eyes for a moment and gripped Samira's hand tighter. When he opened his eyes he realized his senses hadn't fooled him. He recognized the boy that he hadn't seen in ten years, the boy looked just the same now as he had then.

At first, Josh didn't recognize the man standing next to Billy, but only a second later he realized it was Dorn Hale. Josh's head swirled and he felt as though he was in a dream. It was the sight of the third person that made Josh's heart leap from his chest. The man came from behind Dorn, wadded up his hot dog wrapper, tossed it into a trash container, then looked up.

It was his brother.

"Jare," Josh said, his voice quivering.

The two men and the boy looked at Josh, Samira stood quietly.

"Jare," Josh said again.

The look on Jared's face changed, "Josh!" Jared stepped forward and threw his arms around his brother, who was now an inch taller than he. Josh held on to his brother as tight as he could, he didn't want to let go. When they separated, both of their faces were streaked with tears.

"What?" Josh realized the impossibility of this moment. "How?"

Dorn stepped forward and held out his hand, Josh shook it and pulled him in for a hug. Then Josh looked down at Billy. Billy stood with a gleam in his eyes and a smile on his face. The hot dog in his hand had little pebbles littered in a swirl of mustard and ketchup.

39

The five of them sat around the hotel room. Billy and Samira sat on the couch, Jared and Josh sat on the edge of one bed, Dorn on the other. They used torn pizza box lids for plates as they ate their pizza. Billy pulled his piece of pizza away from his mouth after a bite and let the cheese stretch, then he broke the cheese sling at the halfway point, tilted his head up and put the melted mess into his mouth.

The palaver they had as they roamed through the festival and on the drive to the hotel had built up their appetite. Jared and Josh grabbed another piece of pizza in succession while Dorn washed down the last of his crust with an amber lager that Josh had picked up in a growler at a nearby bar. After the initial pleasantries at the festival, they filled one another in on what was happening. When Dorn said they were searching for Raistlin, Josh nearly spit out his beer when he realized he hadn't told them that he and Samira had seen Lance.

As they finished their pizza, Josh showed Jared pictures of their young nephew. Jared leaned forward and looked at the phone screen. He looked at Josh and smiled.

"Mom and Dad just gotta be tickled to death," Jared said.

"It added new life to Mom. She needed it, ever since..." Josh trailed off and looked at Jared.

Jared nodded and lowered his eyes to his makeshift plate.

To change the mood, Josh grabbed the remote and bumped up the volume, then he began clicking through the channels.

Samira pointed to the television, "Stop," she yelled. "Go back!"

Josh clicked back one channel.

"Turn it up, that's Mason!" She scooted to the edge of the couch and leaned toward the television.

"... man has gone missing. Mason Barrow was last seen in his room at the Longfellow Nursing Home. He is believed to have wandered off and suffers from early-onset Alzheimer's."

Dorn stood up as the news anchor went on. An image of the man was in the upper corner of the television screen. He bumped Jared's shoulder, "There he is."

Jared squinted at the picture on the television. It was of an old man with long gray hair and a wiry white beard, then the picture went away and a new story was on. "Holy cow, it is him, isn't it?"

"You guys know Mason?" Samira looked at Jared and Dorn.

Dorn shook his head, "His name isn't Mason, it's Raistlin."

"Raistlin?" She looked confused.

Josh turned the volume down on the television and said in a quiet voice, "Yeah, babe. Raistlin Barrow. It's who they came here for."

Samira chuckled to herself, "This just gets weirder and weirder."

Billy had been watching the interchange with his half-eaten piece of pizza in his hand. The cheese slid off and landed on his leg. "Aw, shucks!" he whispered and quickly looked around to see if anyone noticed.

"We need a plan," Dorn said.

. . .

Two police cars sat outside the entrance of the nursing home. Jared and Josh walked through the front doors of the building and to the front desk.

"We are here for information on Mr. Barrow," Jared said to the woman at the counter.

One of the policemen in the lobby stepped forward as the woman said, "Are you family?"

"Um," Jared fumbled his words. "I'm his son."

"Grandson," Josh cut him off. "We are Mr. Barrow's grandsons."

The policeman stepped in, "Has he wandered off before?" he said. "I mean before he came here. Was it common for him to just wander off?"

"No," Josh said. "Not that I know of."

"Any idea where he might go?" the cop asked.

Josh shook his head.

"Can we exchange numbers?" the cop said as he pulled a notebook from his front shirt pocket.

The phone numbers were exchanged and Jared and Josh headed back to the SUV where everyone else was waiting.

"What now?" Jared asked as he climbed into the vehicle.

"Let's go to his apartment," Samira said. "Maybe there will be a clue there or something. Regardless, Atticus needs fed."

They drove ten minutes to the apartment. Atticus was a bit skittish with all the other people, but soon he warmed up to them. Samira leashed the dog and took him outside. The others peeked around the apartment politely until Dorn found a photo of Raistlin. In the photo, he was sitting next to a much younger Atticus, both looking at the camera. Around them were tools made for leathering, and piles of different quality leathers littered the table and floor.

"He always was a good leatherworker," Dorn said.

"Look at the dog, Dorn," Jared pointed to the picture. "Look how young he is."

"Is this the same dog as…" Dorn pointed to the door Samira and Atticus had exited just a few minutes before.

"Yes, it has to be," Jared said.

"It just doesn't seem possible," Dorn said and set the picture back on the mantle. Just then Samira came back in with the dog.

"Was Raistlin a leatherworker?" Jared asked Samira.

"Mason?" she asked as she unhooked the leash. "Yes, he made a handbag for my friend, Julie."

Josh leaned toward her and whispered, "Raistlin."

"What?" she asked.

"Raistlin," Josh said. "His name is Raistlin."

"Oh yeah," she whispered. "Sorry."

"Did he work for someone?" Dorn asked.

Samira shook her head, "No, I think he had a shop somewhere?"

"You don't know where?" Josh asked.

"No, but…" she looked around the room. A desk sat in the corner littered with papers and envelopes. She walked over and looked at a few, then pulled one off the desk, "Got it."

"Let's go there," Jared said.

As they headed for the door, Josh walked back to the end table by the couch and grabbed the journal that he had peeked at days before.

As they walked out the door, Atticus slipped past the threshold into the hallway of the apartment complex. The door to the apartment clicked shut.

Samira reached down for his collar and said, "C'mon, buddy. You have to stay." She reached for the doorknob, but it was locked. She reached into the pocket of her jean shorts, but her hand came out empty. She checked her back pocket, still to no avail.

"Shoot," she said. "I must have left the key inside."

Josh let out a sigh, "Well, he goes with us, then."

"Wait, we can't..." She started.

Josh held one arm out to his side as he opened the main door of the complex with his other, "What else you gonna do?"

When they reached the SUV, they all piled in, even Atticus. Grunts and groans filled the vehicle as the big Airedale Terrier tried to find purchase on the passenger's thighs. Jared followed the navigation on his phone, and in a few minutes, they were parked in front of a shop. Josh and Dorn walked to the big storefront window, held their hands beside their eyes, and tried to see in.

"It looks like it has been closed for a while," Josh said.

"Yes," Dorn said. "Yes, it does."

Without any more clues, they headed back to the hotel room, this time with tacos from a local takeout. Josh threw his shirt over a camera in the hotel hallway while Billy and Samira snuck Atticus into the room.

40

Josh crawled out of bed and slipped on his jeans and shirt. He used the bathroom, and when he walked out he scanned the scene of the hotel room. It looked like a college party. Lettuce and shredded cheese littered the floor in spots, the trash containers overflowed with cups and taco wrappers, and people were sleeping all over the hotel room. He noticed Dorn was not in the room. He grabbed the journal out of his pack and headed for the door. Atticus shook himself and yawned and stretched. When Josh grabbed for the door, Atticus was at his heels.

"No, buddy. You can't come with me. C'mon, one more hour," Josh said as he led the dog back toward the beds. He patted the spot where he had been sleeping just minutes before, "Up here, buddy."

The dog jumped up on the bed and stretched out next to Samira.

Josh quietly slipped out of the hotel room, made his way to the lobby, and grabbed a coffee. He looked around the dining area but didn't see Dorn. He walked to a door that led to an outdoor patio and saw Dorn sitting at a table. A coffee sat in front of him as he gazed out at the city.

Josh pushed the door open and walked through, "Good morning, Dorn."

The greeting pulled Dorn from his gaze and he looked at Josh, "Oh, hello Josh."

"Bright and early as usual, huh?" Josh said.

"Yep, it never changes. No matter what world I am in."

"Any ideas for today?"

"No," Dorn sipped his coffee. "I haven't a clue."

Josh lay the journal on the table and sat down, he set the coffee off to the side with the notion that if he spilled it, no stains would get on the journal.

"I swiped this from the apartment last night," Josh said.

"And what would it be?" Dorn asked as he looked at it.

"Let's find out," Josh said as he opened the journal. He began reading the first page, which was written in fine handwriting.

January 15, 1992

"Holy crap," Josh said.

Dorn leaned in to speak but Josh held up his hand and continued to read.

The weather here can be unbearable! Yesterday when I arrived the wind whipped the snow so hard it felt like getting poked in the face with dozens of sewing needles at once. And I have never seen so much snow in one place or felt this wicked, cold air. After the storm passed, big machines moved the snow off the streets and had it hauled away— to where? I don't know.

I paid for a map at a fuel station this morning, so I know where I am— not that it matters. I go back to where the stone arch stood, but it is not there. At some point, it should appear, and Dorn will walk through and find me— if The Great Fathers figured out a plan.

Raistlin J. Barrow

Josh looked up at Dorn. "Dorn, Raistlin has been here for thirty years."

Dorn leaned back in his chair, "Oh, Great Fathers, the book was right."

"What book?"

"The Book of Secrets."

"The Book of Secrets?" Josh leaned forward. "I haven't seen that since..."

"Your brother took it from you when you were in Evergreen. He originally thought it was something that should be left behind. Once he was also left behind he felt horrible about it. He couldn't believe he stole from his own brother." Dorn sipped his coffee. He looked at Josh with his dark eyes. "A few nights ago, Billy read out of the book and it said we were thirty years too late. Then the book turned to ash."

"It just doesn't seem possible," Josh said.

"Keep reading," Dorn said as he scooted to the edge of his chair, ready to hear what was next.

Josh flipped to the next page and read.

January 17, 1992

The snow has finally been cleared from the streets, and people are moving about in their coats and scarves. Even though the sun shines, the air is still brutally cold. I haven't ventured far because of the cold, but I am hoping to see a sign or an arch to find my way home.

Raistlin J. Barrow

Josh scanned the next several pages, and then stopped and read:

March 22, 1992

I am not convinced that I will be going to Evergreen anytime soon. I have checked every inch of the area, but there is no sign of going home. Since I have nothing to barter, I think I will have to find work if I want to continue to have a dry place to sleep and something to eat.

Raistlin J. Barrow

A few pages later, Josh read:

March 30, 1992

I have found work that falls into my wheelhouse. There is a leather worker with a shop just a few blocks from here. I have convinced him to let me help. The pay is enough to get by, and that makes me happy.

But I spend my alone time wondering about Tessa, Anastasia, and Cambria. I also wonder what happened at Greystone. I wonder about Dorn. I have been lost since I watched Josh and Billy leave. My heart breaks that I wasn't able to bring Jared home, and I wonder how Cambria handled his death.

I feel lost, but I will continue to live. I will continue to hope. Someday, I will be back in Evergreen with the people I love.

I promise!

Raistlin J. Barrow

Josh flipped through the next several pages in silence. Dorn gazed at the buildings that surrounded the courtyard.

"He seems to touch on the different people and the culture of his new life," Josh said as he kept turning pages. "He also seems to enjoy American literature."

"He is a reader," Dorn said after a quick sip of coffee.

"He mentions Steinbeck, Hemingway, and Harper Lee," Josh said.

One of the doors to the patio opened, and Jared walked out. "Mornin' gents," he said.

"Good morning," Dorn said.

"Hey, Jare," Josh said with his nose in the journal. For a moment, he wanted to mention how oddly nonchalant it was to greet his brother, who had been dead for ten years but stood before him now. His focus was pulled back to the writings.

Josh scanned the pages of the journal, then a squeak came from the gate to the courtyard. Samira and Billy walked through the gate with bags in hand. Atticus followed.

"Hey guys," Samira said. "Billy and I grabbed breakfast sandwiches from Mudgies."

"How'd you get the dog out of the hotel?" Jared asked.

Before anyone answered, Josh spoke, "Hey, check this out." He scooted forward in his seat and read from the journal.

September 25, 1992

This morning, the stone arch I have been searching for finally appeared. I was walking through Riverside Park when I saw the arch in the distance. I began to walk toward it, then I broke into a run. I reached the stone arch and ran through it. Once inside, I slowed to a walk. The length of the tunnel was no longer than a few blocks in Corktown. When I walked out the other side, the sun was warm and...

41

The sun was warm on Raistlin's face as he walked out of the tunnel, but the air held a cool touch. He looked back into the tunnel, but it had changed. It was no longer a dark, straight tunnel. It was a dusty tunnel, although still dark. Raistlin looked around the countryside, but he didn't recognize any of it. Mountains surrounded him, but they were different than the few mountains he was familiar with in Evergreen. He thought maybe he was in the land on the other side of Rickenback Mountain, the land which no man had come back to tell about.

A man walked out of the tunnel with a wide brimmed leather hat on his head and dusty overalls strapped over his shoulders. He wore a cotton button up shirt with the sleeves rolled to the elbows.

The man looked at Raistlin and said, "Good day."

Raistlin nodded and said, "Same."

"You looking for work?" the man said as he took off his hat and wiped his brow with his forearm.

Raistlin shook his head and asked, "How far is Ironwood from here?"

The man gave an odd look, "Never heard of such a place."

"What about Greystone?"

The man shook his head, "Don't know that one either. Closest town to here is San Francisco."

"How do I get there?"

"Follow that river, you'll get there."

...

After sleeping for two nights under the stars, Raistlin realized he wasn't in Evergreen. He took a job working in the mines before he reached San Francisco. They were looking for gold. Raistlin's job was to lead the mules that pulled the carts of dirt out of the tunnels. From there, the dirt was washed down to see if there was gold.

After two weeks of finding very little gold and no pay except two meals a day and a sleeping sack under the stars, Raislin left early one morning.

There were other camps along the way, which the people referred to as claims. The focus of every claim was to find gold. Many times there were arguments about who owned the gold that was found. Several times violence erupted. Raistlin realized he was in the Wild West.

He made it to San Francisco in a few days and slept on a dusty street that night. The next day he ventured around town and realized the year was 1853 and he was in the heart of the California Gold Rush.

The following day he got a job as a cook. He soon realized his love of cooking only extended to doing it for his family and friends. Cooking for dozens and dozens of people, day after day, was not in his best interests.

Two weeks after he arrived in San Francisco, Raistlin found himself in a saloon. He drank a steam beer while a piano player danced his hands across the ivory keys. A man with a round face and a gray beard sat at the bar with a glass of whiskey before him. The man spoke loudly about all of his help wanting to go to the mines or the streams and strike it rich.

125

Once Raistlin had made it to town, he realized very quickly the only successful people in this gold rush were the ones who started their own businesses. The miners with gold in their bags that came to town soon spent all of their findings and headed back out to mine more gold. The business people made money hand over foot, whether it was selling clothing, food, shovels and picks, or running a brothel. It was obvious where all the gold wound up at the end of the day.

Raistlin ordered another beer and listened to the man. Once the man was done ranting and raving about not finding help, Raistlin spoke up. "What business are you in, sir?"

The man looked at Raistlin, somewhat startled that anyone besides the bartender was listening. "Clothing. I make durable clothing for the miners. There isn't anything made today that can hold up as good as my clothing. Why do you ask?"

"I can help you," Raistlin said, then took a sip of beer.

"You're not a miner?" the man said.

Raistlin shook his head, "That trade is for fools. I am currently a cook at the spot two buildings away. I have plenty of experience with textiles."

The man stood up, grabbed his drink, and walked to Raistlin's end of the bar. He set his drink down and put out his hand. "The name is Strauss, Levi Strauss."

Raistlin shook his hand, "Name's Barrow, Mason Barrow."

The two men sat at the bar for hours, talking about everything. During the conversation, Raistlin learned a lot about the state of the country. Hearing the word "America" made him think of his trusty steed, and it made him homesick. Not only was he far away from Evergreen, but he was far away from what he felt was his temporary home in Detroit.

For months, he worked for Levi Strauss, even to the point of helping him run the business. The payouts were great, Raistlin even felt sorry for many of the miners that came to town bragging about finding gold, only to find themselves broke in a matter of days.

None of it mattered to Raistlin, the money nor the gold. Neither of them would be worth anything in Evergreen. However, the more he thought of it, he realized gold would have a place in Evergreen, albeit a bad one. Once gold found itself in the hands of people like Lance Erikson, there would be trouble. Thievery and corruption would be the result and maybe even a war. The only result would be greed, and Raistlin didn't like it.

Raistlin saw his fair share of evil while living in the Wild West. He saw a man get gunned down in the dusty street and drop dead. There were fistfights in the saloons on a daily basis. Women from the brothel tried to get his money in exchange for love. Raistlin always declined, although he would often leave a pair of coins for a lady in exchange for good conversation. His only friends in town were Levi and the bartender, and Levi was often long winded to the point of annoyance.

Raistlin counted the days since he had arrived in the gold rush, and on the one hundred forty-sixth day, he found his way back to Detroit.

After a long day of working with Strauss, he walked down to the bay. Halfway across the bay, a rocky island sat, the water moved swiftly around it toward the Pacific Ocean. As he gazed at the opening of the bay and the vast ocean, he noticed a stone arch on the shoreline. He looked away for a moment, then back, and it was still there. He walked down the hill toward the arch, then he began to run. Tears welled in his eyes with the excitement of finally being able to return to Evergreen. He ran through the arch and into a tunnel. Soon it was pitch black, but he kept running. His heart pounded and he became winded, but he refused to stop. Soon, he saw the light at the end of the tunnel. As he ran, the light became bigger and bigger. Once he was close enough, he was able to make out shapes on the outside of the tunnel. There were buildings, which made his heart sink. He slowed to a walk as he neared the opening. He walked out into the bright sunlight. The skyline of Detroit, Michigan stood before him.

Raistlin fell to his knees and pounded his fists on the ground as tears of frustration fell from his eyes. Once he regained his composure, he walked to his apartment.

A bank sign that he passed showed the date: September 25th, 1992. Not a day had passed in Detroit, although he was in the Wild West for nearly five months. Once he reached his apartment, he wrote in his journal.

42

Raistlin continued to work for the leather maker in Corktown. During the evenings, he frequently stopped at a local bar and had a beer or two, and he often visited the local family-owned restaurants.

As the years went on, Raistlin's hair turned from salt and pepper to gray and white. He let his beard grow to the middle of his chest. While walking on the sidewalk one day, he heard a child tell his mom, "Mom, look! It's Dumbledore!"

In the year 2012, Raistlin bought the leather company from the owner who had decided to retire. Now, he not only made the leather products, he ran the everyday operations of the small business. Business was too slow to hire any helpers, so he continued on his own.

On a dreary day in 2016, a big dog with wiry hair showed up at his shop. Raistlin went out to pet the dog and felt its ribs under the coarse fur.

"You want to come in, buddy?" Raistlin said as he held the door open. They went inside and split a ham sandwich that Raistlin had in the fridge. Raistlin talked to the dog as he worked, telling the dog he couldn't stay at the shop, and wondered who his owner was.

At the close of business for the day, Raistlin walked out of the shop with a book in his hand as the dog followed. The book was a paperback copy of *To Kill a Mockingbird*, a novel Raistlin was on his third time reading because he loved it so much. Raistlin patted the dog on the head and said, "Maybe I'll see you tomorrow?"

The dog wagged his tail.

Raistlin began to walk off as he slipped the book into his back pocket; the dog followed.

"So, you're coming home with me?"

The dog wagged his tail more and nudged Raistin's leg.

"Okay, only until we find out who you belong to. How about I call you Atticus?"

43

Raistlin was a lonely man during the decades he spent away from Evergreen. He always kept to himself, spending most of his time reading or writing in his journal. His social times were having dinner or a brew at a local establishment. He understood the importance of community and loved to support local business owners, but other than that, he was a loner. He longed to be back in Evergreen. It didn't matter how many years stacked up, he never lost the focus of going back to his true home.

When Atticus came into his life, Raistlin spent more time at his apartment as opposed to a bar or restaurant. He spent more time cooking for himself and shared many meals with Atticus.

...

Atticus was a patient dog. He spent the first years of his life on the streets, his first memory was climbing out of a cardboard box and landing on a dusty street. He was immediately separated from his three brothers and one sister once a stranger noticed the box of puppies he had just fallen from. The stranger walked off with the box. Atticus never saw his siblings again.

He was immediately adopted by a young couple. They found him in the streets, felt sorry for him, took him in as their own, and named him Max. He lived the first year of his life under the obedient care of his masters, but before he knew it, he was back on the streets again. The young couple had split and given him away to what they thought was a good home. Just a few months later, he was on his own.

For months, he scrounged for food in the streets of Detroit. The best day of his life was when he met the gentle old man with a gray beard that ran a shop that smelled like his first owner's leather jacket.

. . .

The years had taken a toll on Raistlin. Arthritis in his hands made working with leather very difficult. When he walked, his steps became not much more than a shuffle and his shoulders hunched when he stood. His memory started to fade, and his life in Evergreen seemed like another life from long, long ago.

In 2021, his health declined, and he spent time in and out of hospitals and physical therapy rehab centers. Luckily, he had a wonderful neighbor who took care of Atticus while he was away. He struggled to keep the leather shop open. If he broke even for the month, he was satisfied and kept going.

44

Josh set the journal on the table in front of him. His breakfast sandwich was the only one still wrapped in foil. All of the others had their sandwiches finished and their coffee cups empty.

"God, he's been here for thirty years," he said as grabbed his wrapped sandwich.

Everyone around stood silent, trying to absorb the entire journal that Josh had just read.

"He was here when I was here," Billy said as he gazed off. "He could have been just blocks from me at some point. Maybe I saw him and didn't recognize him. He sure wouldn't have recognized me."

"It doesn't matter, Billy," Dorn said. "We'd still be in the same situation. We have to find Raistlin and get him back home.

Part V: Friend or Foe?

"We have to take a trip," Lance said as he set his horn of mead on the wooden table.

"Where to?" Brenna said as she stood behind Lance.

"Someplace special," he whirled around and straddled the back of the chair.

She leaned down and kissed him, which left the taste of honey on her lips.

"We have to find Raistlin Barrow," Lance said.

"Where is he?" Teagan asked as he ran his hand through his hair, pulling it from his face. Teagan was a new addition to Lance's elite since the beheading of Scud. He had brown hair past his shoulders with a mustache and long beard to match. His green eyes were even more intimidating than his large frame and the tattoos that adorned both arms.

"Not in Evergreen," Lance said.

"How do you know this?" Teagan leaned forward.

Lance was beginning to get aggravated with Teagan's questions. Lance felt he poked his nose in his business a little too much.

"I have connections," Lance said and smiled. "Tomorrow, we will leave."

46

Sally and Emily sat in the sheriff's office and talked. It was one of their weekly meetings. Emily stood up and looked out the window, "Who's that?" She said, interrupting Sally.

Sally looked out the window at a man walking toward the saloon. His brown hair fell over the collar of his leather vest. A chain drooped from his waist, holding a wallet in his back pocket. He walked through the swinging saloon doors and disappeared.

"I'll go over there and see what I can find out," Sally said as she grabbed her brimmed hat.

She entered the saloon and walked to the bar. There were three tables taken, one of them with three women hooting and hollering it up.

"Hey, sweet stuff, come on over here and buy us a drink," one of the women shouted to the stranger who had just entered the saloon moments before Sally.

The man had just taken a seat at the bar. He glanced at the ladies with a small grin, then turned to request a drink from Jenn, the hostess.

"Oh, a shy one. Those are the best kind!" The room filled with laughter from the other two women.

Sally leaned on the bar and gazed at the stranger for a second, she had never seen him until today. After Jenn took the man's order she walked toward Sally, grabbed a glass, and began pouring an ale.

"Good day, Sally. Getting settled into the new duties?" Jenn asked.

"Yes, and I seem to be creating new ones by the day."

"Need anything?" Jenn asked as she topped off the beer mug.

"Nope, just a moment of your time."

"Sure, one second."

Sally walked to the end of the bar opposite the new stranger and looked out the window for a second.

Moments later Jenn was across the bar from Sally. "What's up?"

Sally pulled her gaze from the window and glanced at the stranger, then to Jenn, "Who's this guy?"

Jenn glanced down the bar for a moment, "I don't know." She wore a leather vest over a white cotton shirt. Her blond hair fell partway down her chest, and her blue eyes drew the attention of every man who walked into the saloon. "He came in here yesterday and the day before, never seen him before then. Yesterday I heard him say he was looking for work, but we were so busy I didn't get a chance to ask him anything."

"See what you can find out," Sally said.

"Sure will."

"Thank you," Sally said and grabbed a piece of jerky out of the container on the bar before she headed out.

47

Donte and Dorian circled on the ground and snarled at each other. The three dragons still at Barrow Homestead had been restless since Dorn was gone. Dorian had been agitating Donte for days, poking and nudging him, hoping for a fight. He realized early on that Celeste was dead, and he felt it was Donte's fault.

Donte had ignored the taunting, but this time he turned on Dorian. He attacked in a flash and sliced the side of Dorian's neck, at the same time Dorian's back left claw caught Donte in the side of the face. Blood oozed from each injury.

Zelda had been on edge leading up to the fight. She stayed close to the other two dragons in case of a moment like this. Her face grew fierce as she stepped between the two. She snarled at Dorian and nudged him with her snout. Although Zelda was the smallest of the dragons, she was also the most respected. Most of the dragons backed away from her when things got tough. Regardless, Dorian returned the bump with his snout. Zelda crouched and snarled, ready to attack.

A yelling was heard from one of the masters, it was Tessa.

"Enough!" She yelled.

The dragons stopped immediately, took a step back, and waited. Tessa approached the dragons with no fear. Anastasia was in tow.

Tessa held a broom in her hand and smacked Dorian with it, then turned and smacked Donte. Both dragons took a step back.

"Look at you two!" Tessa screamed. "Would you be doing this if Dorn and Raistlin were here? I think not!" She stood tall as she scolded them.

Hawley was running up the hill from the barn, "I'm coming!" he yelled.

The dragons obeyed their masters. Always. Once their masters were developed in their lives, a dragon held a lifelong commitment to obey them. Obeying more than one master for a dragon was not rare. The only five dragons in Evergreen all had the same masters: Jake, Nana, Raistlin, Tessa, and Dorn.

The lanky old man made it to the dragons, panting. "I'm sorry, Tess," Hawley said. "I let my guard down."

"It's no problem, there is plenty for us to do around here right now," Tessa said.

"They've been on edge for a while. Maybe they needed to get this out of their system," Hawley said as he took his hat off and wiped the leather band on the inside. "Maybe I'll take Dorian out on a training run later this afternoon."

48

"How far did you follow him?"

"I was all the way to where the lane narrows down on the way out of town," Zed said as he politely held his cowboy hat in front of him with two hands.

"The lane that leads to the bridge?" Sally asked.

"Yes'm," Zed nodded. "Looks like he was trekking to Greystone."

"Well, what y'all think he was doing here in Ironwood?" Emily Thorton said as she adjusted the sheriff badge on her overalls.

"Jenn mentioned that he was looking for work. He claims he's good at tending horses," Sally said as she gazed out the window of the sheriff's office.

"Maybe there just ain't any work for a man over there in Greystone," Zed said.

"Maybe," Sally said with a sigh. "It just isn't common for anyone from that town to come this way. They know there isn't much work here, our town is only half the size of theirs. Not to mention, there is a lunatic that controls everyone there. Our new visitor is either trying to get out of Greystone, or he is a spy."

"I can go huntin' after him, maybe get some answers for you, Miss Sally," Zed said.

Sally looked at him and grinned, "I'm not a Miss anymore. Remember?"

"Ah, yes ma'am. You broke the hearts of many men when you married Dorn."

"Pff, quit trying to flatter me."

Zed smiled, then said, "Speaking of hunting, When is your Coonhound gonna have pups again?"

"I'm not sure," Sally said. "That last litter was kind of rough on her. I might wait another year."

"Mabel and Henry are about ready to retire. They just can't keep up with the younger hounds," Zed said. "I'm gonna let 'em eat like royalty and lay around in the grass all day long until they cross the bridge to that next world where they can run and run forever."

"Teddy always says he already crossed a bridge of some sort," Emily said. "Says he lived another life already, he just can't remember much of it. Just an image here and there."

49

"I miss Billy Blaine," Anastasia said as she placed a pair of strawberries in her wicker container. She often used Billy's entire name when she referenced him unless it was just the two of them.

"I bet you do," Cambria said. Cambria stooped down, put a full container of strawberries in the wagon, and pulled out an empty one. They were in a strawberry patch at the base of Rickenback Mountain. Surrounding the patch was a small grassy plain that held the grave markers of the ancestors of the people of Ironwood. Most people believed the graves were nothing but markers, that the bodies were gone and on to the next world. But nobody dared to dig up a grave to find out.

Sawyer cooed at the occasional bird that flew overhead as he rested in a sling contraption around Cambria's neck as she worked. "If it makes you feel any better, I miss Jared. Daddy and Dorn, too," Cambria said.

"Where did they go?" Anastasia asked.

"On a journey."

"Did they go through the Dark Forest again?" Anastasia squinted up at her sister. "That's where Billy got hurt."

"Nope, not this time."

"Where to then? Are they going to Greystone?"

"No," Cambria adjusted the sling to make Sawyer more comfortable. "They're not even in Evergreen this time."

"Did they go to Billy's world?" Anastasia said as she took a bite of a strawberry. She pursed her lips at the slight sourness of the fresh fruit.

"I think they did. You'll have to have Billy tell you all about it when he gets back."

"Are they looking for Daddy?"

"Yes, sweetie. That's the only reason they left."

Anastasia squinted again as she looked up, "Can you keep a secret?"

"Of course," Cambria brushed her free hand lightly over Anastasia's hair.

"Do you think Billy and me will get married someday like you and Jared did?"

Cambria smiled, "Maybe. When I was your age I dreamed of marrying some handsome young man. Since I spent all of those years at Nana and Grandpa's cabin, I wasn't sure if it would ever happen. Then Prince Charming came walking across the meadow one day. I knew right then I would marry him."

"Billy says we were married in another life, in his world. He says he remembers it. He said he saw pictures of me as a child, and I looked like I do now." She pulled the stem off the top of the strawberry and tossed it to the ground. "I don't remember it. But he sure says it happened," she popped the remainder of the strawberry into her mouth.

Soon they were headed back to the homestead, but this time Anastasia had the baby in a sling around her neck and Cambria pulled the wagon full of strawberries.

50

Teagan walked the castle grounds, checking in with the guards as he went. Sky was in the courtyard behind the castle training the children since Lance and Brenna were gone. Teagan sat on a stone bench and watched with a smile. Sky and Teagan were secret lovers. Had they both resided in Greystone, they could be public about their love. Since they stayed under the roof of the castle, Lance decided what couples would be in relationships, and nobody had been chosen for Teagan.

Sky glanced over at him and smiled, Teagan gave a grin and winked at her. Then he looked at the children and frowned.

Teagan hated Lance, so much he could taste it. Years before, rumors began to spread around Greystone that Ivan Erikson had fallen ill. Lance Erickson would be the new leader, the ruler of Greystone. The town had only known him as Ivan's son and a good swordfighter. When the competitions came around every year, Lance won, time after time. Other than that, little was known about him. Much of the town was excited about Lance's rise to power. They hoped he was saner than Ivan. Sadly, they were wrong.

Teagan was witness to the first round of children that were rounded up in the middle of the night. Fathers were beaten and mothers were told to keep quiet as their children were hauled away. Teagan, a young adult at the time, leaned against a stone knee wall that lined one of the cobblestone streets in town as the men on horses pulled screaming children up onto the horsebacks and rode away with them. He took a swig out of his whiskey bottle as he watched. He was unsure what to do. He was too drunk to fight properly, and if he went into the street, he would get trampled by the horses. He smashed the bottle against the stone wall and whiskey soaked the gray grout in between the rocks.

Over the next few years, Teagan did what he could to get closer to the castle. He joined the hunting party and became an avid archer. Soon, he was working within the castle walls, often as the butcher after the hunts. He worked his way up the ranks and Lance Erikson always took note.

Just months earlier, Teagan heard a commotion outside as he butchered several pigs for a roast the following day. He leaned toward the high window from his spot at the butcher's block in the basement and saw the legs of men dancing around in a sword fight. Although his hair was in a ponytail, a lock still fell in front of his face. With the knife in his hand, he pushed the hair away with his thumb, leaving a small streak of blood on his face. Teagan hoped Lance would be killed, he had even considered running out to join the fight, albeit for the other side.

He suddenly became sad when the fit young man with Raistlin Barrow was stabbed. He had never seen him before and wondered if it was Raistlin's son. Then a figure blocked the lights from the sconces and a man landed on the ground. Even before the man swung his sword toward Scud's head, Teagan knew who it was. He had never seen Dorn Hale before, he had just heard stories. The people of Evergreen knew that Dorn was bitter enemies with the Eriksons. Stories of him floated around, making him a legend. Teagan stood in awe as Dorn fought with two swords and shuffled his feet around Scud's head which lay in a pool of blood.

Suddenly, Boris arched his back and walked out of view. Dorn launched an attack on Lance that drove them both out of sight. Then Teagan heard a roar so loud it caused him to drop his knife to the stone floor. He had never seen a dragon before. He had heard them in the distance from time to time, but never this close. The roar shook dust off the joists above Teagan's head. Then Boris came into the cellar screaming with a knife sticking out of his back. Others came to his aid as Teagan looked out the window again. Now, a beautiful woman knelt and helped the man whom Lance had stabbed.

. . .

The following day, Lance had Scud's body thrown in the river as his guards and cronies watched. He said Scud deserved a toss in the river because he was weak.

For Lance, the battle was a win. He had mortally wounded the man he intended to. He would not let the war hero go back to his world and change the past. Now it would never happen, and that would satisfy his gods. But he also lost a man, one of his best. A man who was tried and true from day one. A man who gave everything for Lance's best interests. Regardless, Lance used the loss to strike fear in his followers, and tossing Scud's body into the river was the first order of business.

Just days later, Teagan was questioned and evaluated, finally to be put in as one of Lance's elite. Lance liked him for many reasons, but was a bit unsure about his loyalty. Lance brought him in closer to keep a better watch over him.

. . .

Teagan watched the children in sadness, all of them once stripped from their homes; now they were orphans getting trained by mad people who wanted to start a young army.

With Lance gone for a spell, he tried to find a way into the Ironwood community. He went to town and sat at the saloon, asking if there was work available. He didn't have a plan; he just wanted to cross the river and see what it would take to befriend some of Lance's enemies. He wondered how much of this effort was a waste. As soon as Lance returned, it would be nearly impossible for Teagan to get back to Ironwood.

. . .

He whispered to Sky as they lay wrapped in a deerskin blanket under a pine tree in the far corner of the castle property. At first, they giggled and laughed following their romp under the blanket, but soon he became serious.

"They came and took them all," he whispered. "Just a few at a time. Once every few weeks."

"What does this mean?" Sky whispered back. "What happened to them?"

Teagan looked at her with his green eyes. "They are here."

"What? Where?"

"Right in front of our eyes all the time," Teagan whispered as he ran a hand through her blond hair. "Those children you train in the evenings." He paused for a moment. "Those kids were taken from their homes. There is nothing their parents can do. Lance will kill whoever gets in the way."

Sky gasped, "No, this can't be."

"We can stop him," Teagan whispered. "We can make this right."

"We could get killed!" she whispered.

"It's worth a try," he gazed at her, the moonlight filtered through the tree and glowed on her face.

It was the first time he had confided in anyone about his feelings for Lance and what he thought needed to be done. He and Sky agreed to avoid making anything obvious about their relationship in order to achieve what they now felt was the most important thing in their lives. There would be no more sly smiles toward each other and hardly a word between them. Their late-night rendezvous would be now few and far between.

The night he confided in her, he dreamt:

They had just decided on what they had to do. Make some sort of plan to try to get the children home where they belonged, but to do that meant defeating Lance once and for all. Take him out of power by either capturing him or killing him.

Suddenly, he was tied up, standing on one of the balconies of the castle for all to see. Lance stood before him with a sword in hand. Brenna stood on one side of him, Sky on the other. Sky walked to Teagan and whispered, "You were too easy." She leaned back and looked him in the eyes. "You are so stupid. But I had fun." She winked at him and walked away.

Lance walked up to him and swung the sword.

Teagan screamed and woke himself up.

He worried the entire morning that the dream was true and that he had confided in the wrong person. He checked every corridor as he walked, wondering when he would see Sky.

When he finally saw her, it was nearly midday. She walked down the stone path at the base of the castle talking to two of the servants when they passed each other in opposite directions. Until the last second, she pretended that

149

Teagan wasn't there. Then she glanced at him as they made eye contact. She didn't smile or smirk, but the gleam in her eyes told Teagan that it was all right. Their secret remained.

For several weeks, he made his way to Ironwood to try to find a connection to Dorn Hale or Raistlin Barrow. It seemed as if they were nowhere to be found.

With the fear that Lance would return soon, Teagan felt as though he had to do something. One evening, under the light of a sconce in the cellar, he wrote in the best handwriting he could muster.

The following day, he walked into Ironwood and straight to the mayor's office.

He walked in the door, and a woman sat behind a desk, writing on parchment. She looked up and said, "What can I help you with?"

Teagan walked to the desk with his hands held together in front of him. He looked shy despite the tattoos, long hair, and long beard. "Yes, ma'am." He shifted from foot to foot for a moment, then went on. "It's my understanding that Mr. Dorn Hale is your husband?"

"That's why they call me Mayor Hale," she said as she leaned forward with her elbows on the desk.

"Yes," Teagan smiled, still nervous. "Of course." He pulled an envelope from his vest pocket and held it out for her.

"What is this?" she asked without reaching for the envelope.

"This is a letter for your husband. I can't seem to find him myself."

"Aren't you from Greystone?"

"Yes, ma'am. I am."

"Then what are you doing snooping around Ironwood?" Sally asked.

"The letter will explain that, Mrs. Mayor. I encourage you to give it to Mr. Hale." Teagan said.

150

Sally looked at the folded letter and the wax that sealed it shut. "How can I trust you?"

"I only gave you a letter, Ma'am. I am trusting you to deliver that letter, and I trust that you will."

Sally nodded, "Fine. How much more are you going to be snooping around here?"

"I won't be in Ironwood unless I hear from Mr. Hale."

"Are you sure about that?" Sally asked.

"Positive," Teagan said.

"All right then, I'll see you out."

Pawns of the In Between

Part VI: Pawns of the In Between

Exhausted with leads to find Raistlin in Detroit, they took a quick trip south to Sterling State Park. Jared sat off to the side as Josh video-called his mother from a picnic table. Dorn sat and gazed out at the vast lake with no shoreline visible on the other side. Atticus sat at Dorn's feet, neither of them having seen anything like it.

"Hey, sweetie!" their mother's voice came through the phone.

"Hi, Mom!" Josh said.

"Where are you?"

"We needed some fresh air, so we came down to Sterling," Josh said.

Samira leaned into the phone camera, "Hi, Mrs. Collins!"

"Hello, Samira!"

Jared leaned so he could see the phone screen, but not enough to be seen himself. The mix of emotions stunned him. His heart jumped when he saw his mother but broke at the same time. He remembered the last time he saw her:

it was when he and Josh left on their hiking trip that turned out to be a trip to Evergreen. Now he realized that this moment could very likely be the last time he would ever see her. He wanted to jump in front of the screen and smother her with virtual kisses; he would jump through the screen if he could. Instead, he stayed back, out of sight. She had aged in ten years, a bit more than he anticipated. Crow's feet hugged her eyes, and streaks of gray highlighted her hair. Had he lived, he knew she would look younger than she did now. He knew the toll that the loss of a child had on a mother. He had received letters from the mothers of soldiers he had served with. He felt their pain through their words, and then his mother became one of them, a parent with a dead soldier for a son. Here he was, in the world that he had spent over twenty years of his life. Somewhere in Tall Maple Cemetery, he was buried, a dead soldier with two bullet holes in his face. A victim of a war that neither he nor his parents believed in, but he chose to serve his country regardless. He knew what he was getting into, and this is what he got out of it.

His mother looked happy. Muscles pulled his mouth into a frown and tears welled in his eyes. When Josh and his mother finished the conversation and Josh clicked the screen off, Jared walked away and wiped his eyes.

52

Raistlin woke with his arms spread. Ropes were around each wrist, and he was tied to bedposts. He was in a hotel. A blonde woman sat in the chair near the window, engaged in a match that was playing on the television that hung on the wall. Raistlin had seen her in the past, he just couldn't remember when. Once Raistlin started moving, she looked at him.

"My love," she called out. "The old man is awake."

"Ah," a voice came from the bathroom. "I've been waiting. What a pleasure it will be to have palaver with Mr. Barrow." Lance walked out of the bathroom and wiped shaving cream from his face with a white hotel towel. "Raistlin, do you like soccer?"

"I am not a sports fan," Raistlin said with a hoarse voice, then he coughed.

"I am not surprised. That's okay, your feeble mind wouldn't understand such a complicated sport." Lance tossed the towel on the end of the bed, grabbed the remote off the comforter, and turned down the volume of the soccer game that was playing on the television. He folded his arms and looked at Raistlin. "Do you remember who I am?"

"Unfortunately," Raistlin said in between coughs.

"I am a bit surprised that you remember me. How long have you been here now? Thirty years?" Lance laughed. "Quite a mess you got yourself in. Trying to sneak through my castle grounds. Getting the young lad killed. Winding up here and not being able to find your way home. I'm not sure you could screw up any more than that."

"Are you taking me back to Evergreen?" Raistlin asked as he stared at the ceiling.

"You betcha," Lance said.

"Thank you, Great Fathers," Raistlin said.

"I wouldn't be too prompt to thank them. They aren't getting you back to Evergreen. I am." Lanced walked to the side of the bed and looked down at Raistlin. "And they have failed to get you out of here. I am actually doing their job."

"Then why are you taking me back?"

"Because once the people think that I had put a spell on you and made you an old man in a matter of weeks, they will worship me. You see, in Evergreen hardly any time has passed while you have been here for three decades. But I am the only one that knows that. Nobody knows you have been here that long." The blonde girl in the chair giggled as Lance went on, "They will think it is magic. I will be a greater leader than Tecumseh!"

"Tecumseh was a great man," Raistlin said.

"As am I."

"I beg to differ."

"Your time is short, Raistlin," Lance walked away from the bed and looked out the window. Brenna put her arm around his waist as she sat in the chair next to him. "You don't have long to live. So, I am doing you a favor by letting you die in Evergreen. Then your people can bury you at the base of that stupid mountain."

"So, are you responsible for me being here so long?" Raistlin asked.

156

Lance turned from the window and looked at him, "Do you really think I have that level of power, Mr. Barrow?"

Raistlin didn't answer the question.

"Raistlin, we will make the remainder of your time here as comfortable as possible. The lovely Brenna and I are about to grab a bite to eat. Maybe I will bring you some soup back, old man. In the meantime," Lance pulled out a small container, opened it, took a pinch of powder, and sprinkled it in Raistlin's face. "Nighty night."

53

They got a table for five at a restaurant called Cork and Gable which was a short walk from the hotel. They ordered several appetizers, the brothers sipped on tall draft beers, Samira had a margarita, Dorn had a whiskey, and Billy sucked down a Coke. Jared and Josh talked and laughed. Samira listened and learned more about the Collins family. Billy enjoyed the time out with his friends, and Dorn constantly scanned the restaurant.

Just as everyone was having a great time, Billy came running to the table after a trip to the restroom. "It's him!" He said, pointing toward the entrance. "It's Lance! I saw him when I walked out of the bathroom."

Dorn stood up and looked toward the entrance. "Are you sure?"

"Yes," Billy said in a shaky voice. "It's him."

Dorn looked over at Jared and said, "We have to go."

Jared pulled the credit card out of his pocket and set it on the table. "Josh, pay the bill and catch up with us." Jared began to walk after Dorn, who was headed to the door. Jared turned his head back and said, "Billy, stay with them."

Dorn and Jared ran out the front doors and stopped on the sidewalk. One looked one way, and the other looked the opposite way. People were everywhere, which was normal for game night in Motown.

Dorn saw Brenna from nearly a block away. Her height and blonde hair made her easy to spot. Lance was walking next to her. They followed the couple block after block down Michigan Avenue, and when they passed Trumbull Street, Jared spoke into his phone.

"Josh, go back to the hotel. I'll text you soon. We are following them right now."

A moment later, Jared's phone chimed in his pocket, but he paid no notice.

They walked all the way into the heart of downtown, the buildings towered around them. Lance and Brenna took a right on First Street and walked three blocks before they disappeared into a hotel entrance.

Dorn and Jared stood on the sidewalk and gazed at the hotel. "We need to stay there," Dorn said.

Jared looked around for a moment, then said, "You're right. Let's go."

...

"We're staying at a place called the DoubleTree," Jared said as he spoke to Josh on the phone. "Yes, I think we are almost to the river," he paused for a moment. "No not tonight, we'll keep an eye out. I'll call you if something happens." There was another pause and then he said, "Alright, Bro. I love you."

54

Jared opened the hotel room door after he heard the light knock. "Where's Samira and Billy?" He asked.

"They went down to Fort Street Plaza," Josh said as he walked into the room and held up two bags. "Easier for them with Atticus."

"Cool, where's the food from?" Jared asked as he let Josh walk through the door.

"Motor City Kitchen. I thought I'd fatten you guys up during your short stay here," Josh said.

"Hopefully it's short," Dorn said as he looked out the window. "And not thirty years."

A sad look came across Jared's face, he was now a man torn between two worlds. Josh clapped his brother on the shoulder and said, "C'mon, let's eat. Let's enjoy every moment."

Jared nodded and pulled the bag open to see what was inside.

. . .

As they finished eating, Dorn stood from his chair as he looked out the window. "Jared!"

Jared hopped to his feet from the edge of the bed and joined Dorn at the window.

Lance and Brenna were hurrying an old man down the sidewalk toward the river.

"Something is up," Jared said. "Is that Raistlin?"

"I think so, let's head down there," Dorn said.

After a few seconds of waiting for the elevator, Jared said, "C'mon." He led them to the stairwell and the three of them raced down the stairs as Josh called Samira.

"Head toward the river, we see them," Josh said into the phone and hung up a moment later.

The three of them raced down the sidewalk toward the river; half a block in front of them Lance and Brenna attempted to get Raistlin into a taxi. Raistlin tried to push himself away from them and the cab, but only fell to the ground. Lance pulled Raistlin to his feet and pushed him into the cab after Brenna. Lance slammed his door shut a moment before Jared reached the cab. Lance was yelling something to the driver, but all Jared could make out was, "Riverwalk."

"The Riverwalk! Let's go!" Jared said as he gasped for breath.

They raced diagonally across the intersection of Washington and Jefferson, dodging honking cars as they ran. Once they cut through Hart Plaza, they raced by the big fountain. They passed the police station and made it onto the Riverwalk. Jared looked to his right and spotted Josh in the distance. He waved and began running east along the riverbank. Their shortcut paid off. The traffic downtown was snarled, causing a delay for the cab. The cab appeared half a block before them as it turned onto Atwater.

"I think that's them," Jared said and ran faster.

The cab pulled into the parking lot of the park and Lance, Brenna, and Raistlin climbed out. Lance and Brenna each held one of Raistlin's arms and looked around as the cab pulled away. Once they got their bearings, they began to walk across the paved lot toward the Detroit River.

Jared and Dorn ran up behind the three, Lance turned just in time to get a knuckle sandwich from Jared. The punch was not one Jared would write home about; he was still in a half-dead run and off balance when he took the swing. The hit jerked Lance's head back for a moment, but he didn't sway or stagger.

Lance pulled Raistlin close to him as Dorn approached. What one would think would be a gallant fight amongst experienced combat professionals started out as a game of pushing and shoving in a dusty parking lot.

"Let him go," Dorn said.

"Not a chance," came from Lance.

An old man's voice said, "Dorn, is that you?"

And the pushing and shoving went on.

. . .

Samira sprinted ahead of Josh. Billy followed several lengths behind as he held Atticus by the leash.

Samira smashed into Brenna when she reached the scrum. Brenna, being much bigger than Samira, was hardly fazed by the blow. Brenna's pride took control as she released her grip on Raistlin and squared off with Samira.

Samira launched an attack that took Josh by surprise. Josh knew she was schooled in several areas of martial arts, one being a black belt in Tae Kwon Do, but he had never seen her in action. He watched as she threw swift kicks and punches, which caught Brenna off guard, nearly sending her to the ground. As Brenna retaliated with a barrage of punches, Samira ducked and blocked every one of them.

162

Just a few parking rows away from the females in the sparsely filled lot, the other scrambling continued. Lance had thrown Raistlin to the ground when both Dorn and Jared had tried to separate them. Raistlin struggled to get up, but could not.

Atticus tugged at the leash and Billy tried to hang on and coax the dog back.

Lance stood between the two men with his fists up, waiting for one of them to make a move. Dorn attacked first with punches to the face and kidneys. Lance blocked the face punches but grunted as the punches landed at his torso.

Jared drove in from the side and took Lance to the ground with an old wrestling move he remembered from high school. They grappled on the ground while Dorn tried to get Raistlin to his feet.

. . .

"There it is," Billy yelled as he pointed. Dorn and Raistlin were the only ones to look. Ahead of them, halfway between the far edge of the parking lot and the river, was an arch. Inside the arch, it was pitch black.

Josh, always the peacemaker, waited intently as the two girls fought. He had rarely needed to break up a fight. When his brother fought in front of him in the past, he was always too little to get involved. His brother always told him, "If they ever put me on the ground, just run or they'll put you on the ground next." Josh never had to run when his brother fought.

When Brenna pulled the dagger and pointed it at her rival, Samira bounced on her toes, a sly smile formed on her face. Years of training had prepared her for this moment.

Josh's impatience and peacemaking mentality ruined the moment for her. He jumped in between them and yelled, "No!"

Brenna swiped the knife at him in an arc. Josh jumped away with his arms in the air. The knife cut through the front of his shirt. He stumbled and looked down to see if he was cut. Brenna leaped forward and gave him a push. He stumbled backward onto the sidewalk.

A bus that was going much too fast for downtown traffic sped down Atwater Street. As Josh stumbled from the shove by Brenna, the bus drove over the curb and onto the sidewalk.

Samira lost focus of the fight and screamed as the bus plowed into Josh. Josh did his best to avoid the collision. He tried to dive out of the way, but the front of the bus caught his right leg and sent him spinning. He flew back into the parking lot, and his head bounced off the pavement. He lay still with his leg broken just above the knee.

Samira ran over to Josh as he lay unconscious. Brenna ran to the other fight. Raistlin was back on his feet but was useless with his old age. Jared and Lance had gotten the best of each other on the ground. Dorn grabbed Raistlin and started toward the arch.

"Billy! We have to go!" He yelled. "Jared!"

Brenna jumped on Jared's back with the knife high in the air. Brenna, sensing something behind her, turned toward Raistlin.

Billy, overcome with things escalating as quickly as they did, lost hold of Atticus's leash as the dog kept trying to lurch forward.

Atticus, normally a peaceful and quaint dog, raced forward once he felt his leash break free. He raced toward the debacle, not sure if his master was a part of the chaos. He barked and snarled as he approached.

As Jared wrestled with Lance, he suddenly realized that Lance wasn't in his grasp anymore. Now he was grappling with a furry animal.

As Atticus approached with fury, Lance and Brenna transformed into wolves. Jared rolled off to the side and jumped to his feet, his face bloody and bruised. It was then he realized Josh was down as he heard Samira's screams.

Atticus jumped into the foray with fury. The wolves squared up and met his attack. Atticus, a domestic, peaceful animal, was no match for the furious wolves. They tangled and fought. The big, wiry-haired dog didn't know what to do. The wolves ripped and tore at him. Fur flew into the air and yelps and whines came from the unfortunate canine.

"Atticus," Raistlin whispered.

"Josh!" Jared yelled.

Dorn nudged Raistlin toward the arch and yelled, "Billy! This way!"

Jared began to run toward Josh but Dorn stopped him, "We have to go!"

"No!" Jared yelled and tried to break free of Dorn's hold.

"You have to! You're no good here!" Dorn yelled. "You'll die as soon as the arch disappears."

Dorn dragged Jared toward the arch, and Billy followed as Raistlin did his best to keep up with them.

. . .

"Josh."

"Atticus."

Then the four of them walked into the darkness of the tunnel under the arch.

55

Somehow, they walked for several minutes in the dark without bumping into each other. Jared sobbed and tried to catch his breath while Raistlin whispered, "Atticus" over and over. Their depressing sounds echoed in the tunnel.

A light appeared before them, and soon they walked out of the tunnel and green grass was at their feet. Jared fell to the ground and cried. Billy tried to console him with pats on the back. Raistlin staggered as he looked at the sky and quietly cried out his dog's name. Dorn looked around and took in the scene.

Dorn waited for a moment, then asked, "Where are we?"

"The In Between," Raistlin said with his hoarse voice.

Jared regained his composure and stood.

"What now?" Billy asked.

Around them, rock walls stood on three sides. A grass path only led one way; trees lined each side of the path just before the rock walls.

Raistlin lifted one of his liver-spotted old hands and pointed down the path. "This is the only way."

They walked slowly to account for Raistlin, and they walked in silence. Raistlin and Jared were lost in a daze. Dorn trekked forward. Billy gazed at the surroundings, always curious about what was next.

The walk seemed endless; the only things that changed were the size of the trees or the shape of the rock walls.

Soon, the landscape opened up and the rock walls dwindled to nothing, scattered trees and plains adorned the landscape. They walked for miles, and eventually, Raistlin grew weary. They discussed starting a campfire, but there was no food to cook, the weather was warm, and it didn't look as though darkness was going to come anytime soon. They sprawled out on the ground. Raistlin and Billy slept. Dorn gazed at the sky while Jared paced about the grass. He cussed, he broke sticks over his knee, and at times he kneeled and punched the ground. He often looked back the way they had come as if he was wondering if he could go back to Josh. But he knew that the tunnel back to Josh's world was gone, possibly forever. He knew he would never see his brother again.

Hours later, Raistlin woke. Billy still slept with his shirt pulled over his head to block the sunlight.

"Anyone hungry?" Jared asked.

Raistlin and Dorn nodded.

"Billy!" Jared said.

Billy pulled his shirt down and sat up, "What?" He looked around, trying to figure out where he was. "Oh," he said. "I thought I was back home, on LaBrosse Street. In the 1960's." He stood up, stretched, and yawned.

"What can we eat around here?" Dorn asked.

"I don't know," Jared said as he gazed into the distance. He pointed, "Let's head to that group of trees over there."

They walked long enough to get lost in their own thoughts.

Jared couldn't stop thinking of his brother. He knew Josh was gravely injured back in Detroit, possibly even killed. What would his mother and father do, losing both sons? He tried to push the thoughts from his mind, but it seemed impossible.

Raistlin held the group to a slow pace but none of them seemed to be in a hurry. The weather was nice and the company was good, so they continued on their way with no flack.

Soon, they were at a group of trees. They heard the happy sounds of children and the occasional crack of a baseball bat.

Billy led the way through the sparse trees at a quicker pace than before. "I think I know this place," he said.

They cleared the trees to a baseball diamond. A few rows of stands sat behind the backstop, and children played on the field, filling all the positions of the American pastime.

"Look," Billy pointed to a concession stand. "Let's eat!"

"Where are we?" Raistlin asked as he looked around.

"This is the In Between, remember?" Jared said.

"Oh," Raistlin said. His condition wasn't improving. His gait had slowed, his gray hair hung in his face, and he seemed to comprehend the things that were happening only part of the time.

They went to the stand for hot dogs, popcorn, and colas.

They sat in the bleachers and scarfed their food, but Raistlin ate his slowly. He sipped on his cola and said, "You know how long I was in Billy's world?"

"We have a pretty good idea," Dorn said before taking another big bite. Mustard and ketchup slid off the back of the hot dog.

"What an adventure, huh?" Raistlin said. He had only taken two bites of his hot dog and the others were nearly done. "I'd been there so long. Now, I just want to go home. The Great Fathers really messed this one up, and they probably don't even realize it."

"I think they made a mistake," Jared said. "You fellas have explained to me in the past how getting from Evergreen to my world was like throwing darts with a blindfold. I think in the mix of trying to get Josh, Billy, and myself home, they just couldn't nail all of it."

"Jared," Raistlin's voice was stronger now that he had sustenance in him, but his face still looked rough. "How did you get here?"

Jared looked him straight in the eye, "Your daughter saved me." He glanced over at Dorn, "Dorn as well. Without either of them, I would have died in Evergreen."

Raistlin closed his eyes and whispered, "Cambria."

"You may have a grandchild when we get back," Jared reached out and put his hand on Raistlin's shoulder. "You'll be a grandfather soon. Let's get back to Evergreen and get you healthy."

"I'm too old to be healthy," Raistlin groaned. "It's been too long. You can't fix the old people. I don't have much time. We need to get back to Evergreen, it's been so long it seems like a dream to go back."

Jared patted his shoulder with a light touch.

"Look," Billy said, pointing. "The arches!"

They all looked and two levels of stone arches stood on the other side of the baseball diamonds. They spread out in a semicircle, and a stone stairway on each end was the access to the upper level. The arches stood, one after the other. The darkness inside each arch gave them a blank stare.

"What is all that?" Dorn asked.

"It's the heart of the In Between," Billy said as he held a few kernels of corn in his hand. "It's a world of magic."

"This is what Lance designed?" Dorn asked.

"So he claims," Raistlin said with a hoarse voice.

169

"And rebuilt," Dorn said.

"This is the labyrinth," Billy said. "All of these places like this baseball field lead to other things to do. Once you are in a new place, there are several options to go elsewhere. Once you travel to a few places, it's tough to find your way back if you don't pay attention." He took a sip from his cup and went on, "There is so much to do. Josh and I flew airplanes, swam in the Dead Sea, even fought dragons."

"World War II, the Civil War, even the Napoleonic Wars. There is something for everyone," Jared said.

"How do we get to Evergreen," Dorn asked.

"There's only one way to find out," Jared said.

56

They all stood before the two arches. One read, "Josh Collins," the other read, "Billy Blaine."

"What happens if I go through Josh's tunnel right now?" Jared asked.

"Josh would be twelve. You may be dead or alive. If you are alive, you may be dead soon," Billy said. Then he looked at Jared, "Sorry. That was kind of gruff."

Jared gave a hint of a smile, "All good, buddy."

"I think our best gamble is to go up the stairs," Billy said.

As they made their way to the stairs, Billy talked. "I drew maps of this place when I was a kid. Actually, I drew them as I grew into a grown man. I had dreams about this place, year after year." Dorn helped Raistlin up the steps as Billy continued, "It was hard to remember what was what, but then a new dream would come to me during the night. Then I would draw another page of the labyrinth. I don't know if it was all correct or not, but it was fun. I never knew what happened to those drawings."

Once they were on the top level, the four of them looked at the arches. The arches stood side by side, one after the other; They made an entire semi circle. A granite floor spread out before the arches. At the other end of the arches was another stairway that led back down to the ground level. A short stone wall stretched behind them from one stairway to the other.

Jared took a step back and leaned against the short wall as he looked at the arches. "Pick your poison," he said.

Dorn looked at the arches with his usual stoic face. Raistlin swayed slowly back and forth. He looked like a man that was at the end of his road. His gaze showed no interest in what was happening. Billy crumpled his popcorn bag and tossed it over his shoulder as he chewed the last few kernels.

"The last thing," Billy said through a mouthful of popcorn. He swallowed, then continued, "The last thing Josh and I did together here was ride in a hot air balloon. Maybe it means nothing." He glanced back and forth at the other arches. "But you never know."

"Hot air balloons it is," Jared said. He stepped to Raistlin, took his arm, and headed toward the arch they had picked.

They stopped when they reached the other end of the tunnel. There were a few hot air balloons in the sky. Billy looked up at one and put his right hand to his forehead to block the sun. The balloons were colorful. One had stripes going up and down, and another had them going horizontally. There was a solid blue balloon that almost matched the clear sky. There was also a tye-dye balloon.

"Those are just like the balloons at the wedding," Dorn said. "Except bigger."

They walked to the stone wall. Below them, beautiful green grass spread out for acres. On the ground, a stone's throw away, a deflated balloon was spread out over the grass. The balloon was patterned with a colorful swirl that started at the top and worked its way down. Attached to it was a big basket made of strips of hardwood weaved in and out. Mounted to the top of the basket was a metal device.

172

They walked down the stairway and over to the balloon lying on the ground. Dorn turned around and his eyes got bigger and his jaw dropped slightly. Jared and Billy turned to see what Dorn had seen. Raistlin leaned forward against the big basket, not bothering to turn around like the others.

"One step into the labyrinth," Billy said.

The three of them looked at two levels of arches in a semicircle pattern just like the ones at the baseball diamond.

"The bottom ones are for the kids to go home," Billy said. "And the top ones are to go do something fun."

"Hey, Billy?" Jared said.

"Hmm," Billy said as he gazed at the stone structure with the stairs and arches.

"How many kids do you suppose got lost and never made it home?" Jared asked as he turned his focus from the arches to Billy. "How many kids just went crazy with all of the fun things to do and didn't keep track of where they were going? Like getting lost in a forest." He looked back at the arches. "Do you think some of them didn't make it back home?"

"Jeepers, Jared. I never thought of that."

"That's it," Raistlin's gravely voice said.

"What's that?" Dorn asked.

"That's where the children come from," Raistlin's head drooped down as he leaned on the basket. "The children Lance has held hostage."

"What's this all about, Raistlin?" Dorn asked.

"I saw things," he lifted his head, his gray hair covering much of his face. "Here, in the In Between. I saw these things thirty years ago, right before I went to Billy's town." He turned to look back at the others. "He has children held hostage, in the basement of his castle. Many of them are from Greystone, but there are too many there to make up all the kids from Greystone. The rest are from here. Jared, you have just made a huge discovery." Raistlin turned his head toward Dorn and said, "We have to save those children." Then Raistlin fell forward against the big basket.

Their efforts to catch him were too late as Raistlin rolled off the side of the basket, fell to the ground, and lost consciousness.

Dorn stood up from trying to catch Raistlin and looked to where the arches stood moments before, "Great Fathers," he said.

Jared and Billy looked to where he was looking, and saw the arches were gone. Only a green pasture spread out before them.

"What the?" Jared said.

"They're gone," Billy whispered at the same time.

The three of them stood in the sunlight and looked at the vacancy in the distance while Raistlin slept at their feet.

"There is only one way to go," Dorn said and looked at the empty basket.

"But, which way do we go?" Jared said.

"Wherever the wind takes us," Billy said as he walked toward the large deflated balloon on the ground.

. . .

Soon, they were in the air. Billy controlled the altitude of the balloon with adjustments to the large flame. Raistlin was back on his feet and leaned against the side of the basket. The other two gazed over the land, looking for anything that may be important to them.

The landscape constantly changed as they soared. Sometimes forests seemed so close to the bottom of the basket that Billy felt as though the trees were big pillows of green leaves and he could jump out and land on them like a bean bag chair. Other times, they flew over congested cities that reflected the hustle and bustle of its residents. They all relaxed the most when they flew over the green plains that were spotted with broad trees. A river wound through the

174

landscape and the wildlife went about its business with no attention to the big balloon that flew above their heads across the sky. Then, for a long spell, they flew over a huge body of water.

"What ocean do you think this is?" Billy asked as he looked up at Jared.

Jared glanced down, "I don't know. The Atlantic? Who knows."

"Maybe it's the Aegean Sea," Raistlin said.

Jared and Billy looked at each other and shrugged their shoulders at the same time.

"Odysseus may be down there," Raistlin said. "Maybe he can help us on this journey."

Jared looked at Billy with a blank stare. Billy gazed over at Raistlin and smiled.

Soon, the sea ended, and they flew over rocky terrain filled with conifer trees and jagged mountains. Before them, above a huge plateau, the sky was full of dark clouds and lightning danced above the horizon.

"Is that the Dark Forest?" Billy asked.

"No," Dorn said. "But we can't go there." He looked down at Billy, "Where can you land this thing?"

Jared pointed to the bottom of the rock wall that held the plateau, "Right there, Billy! There's a spot to land."

Billy nodded and cut the feed to the flame. He looked over the side of the basket. A grass area sat at the bottom of the sheer walls like a peninsula in a body of water. He let the balloon continue to drop; the air currents guided it toward the big green target. He fired the flame a few times as the balloon glided toward the open area.

The unpredictable wind currents that happen in a semicircle of sheer rock walls caused Billy to misguide the landing, and the big basket struck the ground harder than anticipated. At first, it scraped the ground, then it soared a few feet and came back down and hit the ground so hard it tipped over.

The basket dragged across the grass after it tipped. Dirt and grass flew as the passengers tumbled onto each other. Raistlin groaned in pain while the others tried to take their weight off him once the basket was stopped. They helped Raistlin out of the basket as the balloon deflated to a flat teardrop on the landscape.

The sun was hidden behind the rock wall, causing their area to appear as dusk. They all stood around the tipped basket and looked at the surroundings. Rock walls jutted up around them on three sides. In the center, at the base of the walls, a cave opening stared at them with its open jaws.

They inspected the opening of the cave, and once they realized that their only way out of their predicament of rugged terrain around them was to go through the cave, they decided to camp for the night.

Later, Billy and Dorn lay awake under the stars. Jared had already dozed off.

"Will I be able to get back to Evergreen with you guys?" Billy asked.

Dorn crossed his arms at his waist as he lay on the ground and said, "As long as we're under the same sky, everything's going to be all right."

57

They woke at dawn. Billy yawned, looked at the morning sky, and smiled. Jared lit a fire by striking together two flint rocks he found in the rugged terrain. The sole reason for the fire was to have torches for their trek through the cave. They had no weapons to hunt with, and Jared took notice that the game in the area was scarce.

By the time the sun was high enough to beat down on them, they were ready to venture into the cave. Jared had taken his shirt and made a shoulder sling to hold more branches that could be used as replacement torches. They headed into the cave with torches in hand. The torches were made from the thickest branches that Jared could break over his knee.

Dorn led the way, setting the pace only as fast as Raistlin could walk. He held his torch high as they all walked into the dark cave. At first, the ceiling of the cave was a vast, dark purple. Even the four torches could not help to decipher how high the ceiling of the cave really was. Eventually, the ceiling lowered enough that the jagged rocks above them were visible. From the occasional crack in the rock above, small white stalactites the size of miniature pinecones poked down toward the floor.

The cave offered them options from time to time as the path split in two. One of the splits led to a dead end, so they turned back and took the other route. They stopped and lit new torches; Jared was careful to light the new branches on the knotty end so the flame would last longer.

They continued to walk. The path of the cave ventured up and down while it also curved left and right through the mountain. Water drips seemed to amplify over the scrapes of their shoes on the stone floor, but the flames near their heads filled their ears the most. The sounds of the flames were like distant, barely audible waterfalls.

Dorn turned and said, "Raistlin, you need a rest?"

"No," he panted. "Not yet. Keep moving."

A clicking was heard over their light footsteps. It was a mix of clicks and what sounded like bird chirps. At first, they could only hear one, then they heard several as the sounds grew closer to them. Soon, the cave was full of bats. The small flying mammals raced by them with acrobatic agility. The four travelers waved their torches with one hand and covered their heads with the other. It was the most life they had seen out of Raistlin since they found him. The bats flew by them, some swerving between them as the bats raced through the cave. Then they were gone as quickly as they had arrived. Not one of the party was touched by the bats, but the air from the flapping wings and the close chirps and clicks rattled them. They stopped and took a break, starting a fire to produce more torches.

Once the fire was blazing, Billy spoke up, "Hey look! What's that over there?" He pointed toward the next bend in the cave. The dance of the flames made it tough to focus on the object that he pointed to. Something leaned against the wall.

Jared stood and walked to get the object. He sat cross-legged when he came back. He set a roll across his lap that was lashed with leather twine. He untied the knots and began to unroll several sheets of parchment. He scooted

178

back and flattened out the sheets in between the fire and himself. The left side of the pages was bound together with more leather twine so the pages could be flipped like a book.

Billy leaned forward, "That's my," he paused and pointed. "Those are my drawings."

Jared glanced at him for a moment, then looked back at the drawings. The top page had a charcoal drawing that looked somewhat like a blueprint drawing, the images drawn from a birds-eye view.

"Boy," Billy said. "Someone really doctored these up, and I didn't tie all these together with those leather laces. But," he paused for a moment. "These drawings are mine."

Jared studied the first drawing as Billy pointed out a few things. Then Jared flipped to the next page. Dorn scooted closer and looked at the maps as Raistlin dozed off while sitting up. After flipping through the entire set, Jared rolled up the drawings and tucked them inside his belt. He pulled torches from the fire, one by one, and handed them out.

They trekked again; before long they were out of the cave and they stood in bright sunshine. Before them stood another set of arches in a horseshoe shape. Jared pulled the drawings from his belt and opened them up. After a quiet conversation with Billy and flipping the pages back and forth, he stuffed the drawings back into his belt.

"I think we are about to fly some airplanes," Jared said. Jared and Dorn helped Raistlin walk while Billy led the way. They walked through the appropriate arch and walked into bright sunshine on the other side.

Airplanes stood in a grass field, and a thin runway cut through the middle. They walked to the base of the steps, gazed at the landscape, and then turned back to nothing but vast scenery. The arches were gone.

"What just happened?" Jared asked.

"Whoever Lance has helping him is playing games with us," Dorn said.

"How can those arches just disappear?" Jared asked.

"Anything can happen in the In Between," Raistlin said. "We have our Great Fathers. Lance has his higher powers as well."

"What do we do now," Jared asked.

"We learn how to fly those airplanes," Raistlin said as he leaned against the knee wall.

58

They approached a pair of airplanes that were both two seated biplanes.

"I've flown these before," Billy said.

Jared stopped walking, "Are you serious?"

Billy stopped, looked up at him, and nodded, "Yeah, with Josh. We didn't fly these two seaters, and ours weren't biplanes. Can't be that much different."

Jared shrugged and they continued to the planes. Jared turned to Dorn, "You can stick with flying dragons. Let me and Billy handle this."

Dorn looked at him, his dark eyes gave a bewildered look.

"Trust me on this one," Jared said. "Go with Billy."

After Jared and Dorn helped Raistlin into his seat, Billy and Dorn climbed into their plane. Leather helmets and goggles were donned by all of them. Once Raistlin was set, he leaned his head to the side and dozed off. The others placed headsets on their heads, fired the engines of their planes, and inched forward down the runway.

"Billy, where are we headed once we take off?" Jared yelled into his microphone.

"Beats me!" Billy yelled. "We'll figure it out when we get up there."

In a matter of moments, both planes were climbing into the clear sky. They leveled off at a few hundred feet. The green grass below them disappeared as trees took over the landscape below them. A blue ribbon of water cut through the forest and curved its way back and forth into the distance. The cooler air at their elevation swirled around them in the open air cockpit.

Jared pushed the button to activate his radio so he could talk to Billy in the other plane. Before he spoke, he felt three quick vibrations that were accompanied by popping sounds. He looked to the right and another popping sound came as a little round hole appeared on the airplane wing. Jared looked over his shoulder and saw two monoplanes approaching quickly, gunfire flashes appeared behind the propeller of each oncoming plane.

Jared pushed the button and yelled into his mic, "Billy, they're shooting at us! We need to dive and get closer to the treetops."

"Are the bullets real?" Billy yelled. "This isn't supposed to happen in the In Between."

The monoplanes were faster and more agile than the biplanes, and they caught up quickly. As the biplanes angled toward the ground, the monoplanes aimed upward, then they came back down and unloaded a barrage of bullets toward the helpless biplanes. A line of bullets tore through one of the wings of Billy's plane. The sounds of screeching metal were heard over the sound of the engines as Billy's wing tore away. The plane tumbled out of control and smashed into Jared's plane. Both planes tumbled out of the sky and into the trees below.

. . .

Jared's plane was a crumpled mess lying on its side when he unbuckled himself from his seat. He could hear Raistlin in the seat behind him groaning. Jared awkwardly climbed from his seat onto the ground. He walked to Raistlin and began to unbuckle him.

182

Raistlin held his left arm and grimaced in pain.

"Let me see," Jared said quietly.

Raistlin held out his arm. It was bent at an awkward angle between the wrist and the elbow.

After everything Jared had experienced in the war, the broken bone didn't faze him. He kept a straight face and said, "Okay, we'll have to take care of that arm. Let's get you out of here."

Once he had Raistlin resting on the ground, he gently leaned him back against the fuselage of the plane. "Stay here," Jared said. "Hold onto your arm. I have to go find those guys."

Jared took off through the woods looking for the other plane. He yelled their names as he walked. After a few minutes of walking, he heard Dorn's voice.

Jared yelled back. Soon they were taking part in the most serious game of Marco Polo Jared had ever played in his life. He followed Dorn's voice then the airplane caught his eye and Jared stopped in his tracks.

Unlike Jared's plane, Billy and Dorn's plane never made it to the ground. It was stuck in the treetops, inverted. Both Dorn and Billy looked down at Jared while they hung upside down strapped in the plane seat.

"Well, that was about the scariest thing I've ever been through," Billy said.

Jared let out a deep exhale, "How do you guys suppose you're getting down from there?"

"We were going to ask you the same question," Dorn said. "These straps are hurting my shoulders."

"Well, don't unbuckle them just yet," Jared said. He looked around for a moment, "Let me see what I can do."

He found a strong vine that went all the way up the side of a tree. He tested it by climbing up it a few feet. Once he knew it would hold his weight, he pulled his knife and began to cut it. After several minutes, the vine was severed and he tied it around his waist. He began to climb one of the trees closest to the airplane. He climbed as high as he could, then untied the vine from his waist. He wound up as much of the vine as he could like a cowboy gathering a rope. He tossed the vine over the airplane, but it slipped off the side. The end of the vine went to the ground and it hung from its original tree, too far away for the plane passengers to reach.

Jared climbed down from the tree, retied the rope to his waist, and tried it again. This time, luck was on his side as the vine draped across the body of the plane and fell down toward the ground. The end of the vine hung several feet off the forest floor. When Jared climbed back down, he looked up at the other two and said, "If you can grab the vine and somehow unbuckle yourself without letting go, maybe you can shimmy down."

Dorn grabbed the vine and handed it to Billy. "Here take this," he said. "Pull it taut." Dorn shifted forward in his seat. "Now, I'm going to hold on to you. I need you to unbuckle yourself and hold onto the vine. I'll hold you from back here. When you are free, you'll have to climb down the vine."

Billy grabbed the rope and pulled it tight. His breathing grew shallow, and he said, "Well, this is the second scariest thing I have ever done. This is scarier than that time I went to Cedar Point."

"Billy," Dorn said. "Look at me."

Billy turned and looked at Dorn. Their hair stood straight from their heads because of hanging upside down.

"Don't be scared," Dorn said. "This idea will work."

Dorn's serious look and dark eyes made Billy feel comfortable again, and he said, "Yes, sir."

Jared could hear them talk and move around in the cockpit as he gathered leaves and pine needles and placed them directly under the rope. He knew a fall from the height of the airplane as it hung in the trees would be fatal. He gathered as many leaves, twigs, and needles as he could until he had a pile that was halfway up his thigh.

Dorn's directions to Billy worked, and soon Billy was climbing down the vine. Once he reached the end, his feet dangled above the ground by several feet. Jared reached up, grabbed his legs, and helped him down.

Dorn maneuvered in the cockpit as he hung onto the vine. Soon, he was climbing down the makeshift rope as well. When he was halfway to the ground, the vine broke where it was draped over the body of the plane. Dorn fell in a horizontal position, his back toward the ground.

He landed with a loud grunt, but the pile of forest debris did its job. Dorn was unscathed as Billy and Jared helped him to his feet.

59

They set Raistlin's broken arm with two branches and a long strand of thin vines. Jared told Billy to start a fire, then he wandered off into the forest.

When he returned, the fire was crackling, and Billy was breaking branches over his knee. Raistlin rested against the airplane, his head was leaned back and his eyes were closed. Dorn had the maps out, and he looked them over. Jared went to the plane and looked around the cockpit, then he opened a few compartments on the outside of the plane. He found a small tin can and walked to the river. When he returned, he put the tin of water as close to the fire as possible. He pulled some roots out of his pocket and began to shave the edges of the roots into the water.

"What do you have there?" They all gave a surprised look at Raistlin when they heard his voice.

"I'm making you a little something to help with the pain, and help you sleep, too," Jared said. "One of Cambria's recipes. A dash of turmeric, a little valerian, and top it off with chamomile once it starts cooling off."

"Hey," Dorn said as he looked back down at the drawings. "Take a look at this." He flattened a page in the leatherbound parchments. Billy scooted next to Dorn, and Jared looked on as he continued to shave the roots into the warming water.

"This looks to be the only drawing that doesn't have 'airplanes' written in these spots where all the arches stand." He ran his finger along the entire semicircle.

Billy nodded.

"So, does that mean this map is actually where we are?" Dorn asked. "There is no option to go to the airplane world or whatever you call it. So, if that option doesn't exist, that means this map is the airplane part. When we find the arches, none of them will say 'airplanes' because we are already here."

Jared nodded, "Makes sense." He folded his pocket knife, put it away, and stuffed the roots that remained back into his pocket.

"So, look over here," Dorn moved his finger to another part of the parchment. "It's very light, but it looks like a river comes from the edge of the parchment, then leads to a pool of water. Right at the center of this half circle."

Jared leaned forward and looked, then he grabbed the drawing and tilted it to the flame for more light. "Yeah, I can see it," he said. "Look, it looks like there are trees drawn here, too."

"So," Dorn said. "The end of the river might take us to the next set of arches."

Jared nodded.

"I think we have to see where the river takes us. Floating is our only option," Dorn said and nodded toward Raistlin.

Jared nodded, understanding what he meant. "So, we build a raft." He looked up at the waning light. "Let's do it in the morning."

. . .

They walked to the river and gathered long tree branches and vines.

187

"Do you remember doing this?" Jared smiled as he looked at Billy. "Before we went to the Dark Forest."

Billy was helping Jared lash the logs together. He stopped for a moment as he thought. He smiled, "I do remember! I remember Raistlin saying there should have already been a raft there on the riverbank."

"Remember," Jared said. "Fitz was a step ahead of us, that's how you got hurt in the pit. He took the raft across the river so he could stay ahead of us."

Billy sighed, "That's just sad that Fitz had to be evil like that."

"Who would have thought there would be evil like that in Evergreen? I thought evil like that only existed in our world." Jared said.

Billy nodded, paused for a moment, and went back to his task.

They made the raft large enough to hold the four of them. They placed Raistlin in the middle, and Dorn and Jared stood on each side with long sticks to push off the bottom. Billy sat on the forward edge of the raft and watched for any rocks or logs that they may hit.

The cruise down the river was slow and easy, and much more efficient than walking the riverbank. When the sun was high in the sky, they banked the raft and started a fire on the shoreline.

"When are we going to eat?" Billy asked as Jared shaved more roots into a tin of warming water.

"I'm not sure, Billy," Dorn said. "We are lacking any tools to hunt with, even primitive tools. We could make them, but that would take a lot of time. Who knows, we might be in Evergreen later today." He stood up and dusted off his pants. "You just have to weigh your gambles."

They gathered on the tipsy raft and started floating down the river again. By the time afternoon came, clouds started rolling in, darkening the landscape. Soon, the sky started to grumble and streaks of lightning shot across the clouds. The rain started to come down so hard it was as if they were in a monsoon.

188

Dorn spotted a rock outcropping and pointed, "Up ahead."

They pulled the raft to shore and gathered under the rock ledge. It was dry under the ledge, but there were no dry branches around to use for firewood. The thick clouds and heavy rain blocked out the sun and soon it was dark. An occasional lightning flash was the only illumination under the ledge. Water worked its way to the bottom side of the outcropping and began to drip on them. They curled up on the rock floor and gave their best shot at sleeping. Even Raistlin had trouble sleeping since his medicine had worn off.

. . .

The sun broke through the trees that dripped from the night's rain. They woke and stretched. Raistlin had dark circles under his eyes. With no food or fire, they didn't waste any time and took the raft back down the stream.

Soon, the sun was beating down on them. A light breeze blew down the river. Raistlin snored, sprawled out on the raft. Billy laid belly down on the front of the raft, supposedly watching for rocks below the surface, but mostly daydreaming. Jared and Dorn pushed their long sticks off the rocks to keep them floating down the middle of the river. They both took in the surroundings and enjoyed the peace as they drifted.

As the day wore on, the river began to grow wider. The current lulled, and the raft ride was smoother. The river opened into a small lake, and soon Jared and Dorn's poles couldn't touch the bottom. They set their poles on the raft and sat, looking at the other side of the lake. A stone structure was there.

"There's our next passage," Jared said in a soft voice.

"We should double check those drawings," Dorn said.

Jared nodded. "When we get to shore," he said.

As the light breeze directed them to shore, the stone structure began to look more familiar. It was the same as the other structures they had seen. A semi circle of arches, all leading to different places.

In front of the structure, three children sat in the grass. They looked to be talking with one another. The raft came close to the shore, and Billy jumped out and pulled the raft to the bank.

They woke Raistlin and helped him off the raft. He walked onto the grass and turned back to the lake. He pointed to the shoreline in front of them, "Food."

"Where?" Jared asked as he supported Raistlin on one side, and Dorn supported the other.

"Right there, on the shoreline," Raistlin was still pointing. "You can eat the stalk, just don't eat the brown, fuzzy part."

They walked Raistlin higher up the bank and let him sit.

The other three went back down to the shoreline and began to break apart cattail stalks. They scrubbed them in the water, then stuffed them into their pockets.

"Jared," Raistlin said with his weak voice.

Jared turned and looked at him. Raistlin waved him over with a weak hand. Jared walked over and squatted beside him. "Those kids," Raistlin said.

Jared leaned so he could see the kids, "What about 'em?"

"I can hear them. They are lost." Raistlin turned his head to look at the children, then back to Jared. "They can't find their way. If they don't get out of the In Between, Lance will kidnap them and take them to his castle. These kids will never go home again if they don't get out of here."

Jared looked at the children again, then nodded and said, "I see." He stood up and turned to the water. "Billy!"

Jared waved Billy over when Billy looked up.

They chatted for a moment, then Billy grabbed the drawings and they walked to where the children gathered. Jared let Billy do the talking.

"Are you lost?" he asked.

All three children nodded their heads.

"Where you from?" Billy asked.

Instead of geographic locations for answers, they said, "1922."

"1888."

"2042."

Billy looked at the kid who gave the last response, not sure if he believed him.

Soon, Billy and Jared hunkered over the maps with the three children. Five people who had lived on Earth at some point over a span of more than one hundred and fifty years now gathered in the same spot in a magical world.

Some think of magic as special and forgiving, but sometimes magic just means impossible. Once the children understood the In Between, they no longer questioned it. It was something that was taken in stride. The In Between seemed impossible to most people, but the children didn't care. They looked at it as magic.

As Dorn kept gathering cattail stalks, Jared and Billy continued to help the three children try to navigate their way out of the In Between.

Once the children went their own way, Dorn, Jared, and Billy stood by Raistlin and munched on cattail stalks. One by one, they stooped around Raistlin and looked at the drawings. They spoke quietly, and soon the maps were rolled up, lashed, and tucked away.

Moments later, they were walking through another arch, this one labeled "Blizzard." When they reached the end of the tunnel, snow swirled around the entrance, and the wind howled.

"Great Fathers," Raistlin said. "This is how it was when I arrived in Billy's world."

They walked into the swirling snow. Dorn led the way while Jared and Billy helped Raistlin walk. The drifts were almost to their knees in the deep spots. The icy snow pierced their faces like needles. All of them had to close their eyes almost completely shut or the wind and snow were too painful. Raistlin had grown accustomed to wearing sneakers in his old age, and his feet were paying the price as they grew cold and wet very quickly. Billy was in the same boat since he wore his tennis shoes when they walked through the tunnel to Detroit. Dorn and Jared both donned leather boots made by the cobbler in Ironwood.

"Are you sure this was the right way to go?" Billy yelled to Jared over the wind.

"You saw the maps, Billy," Jared yelled back as he put his arm tighter around Raistlin's waist. "This was the only path to Evergreen."

"What if the maps are wrong?" Billy yelled.

"You are the one that drew them up, remember?"

"What if I was wrong?"

"It doesn't matter!" Jared yelled.

Dorn stopped. The others stopped behind him. Dorn turned around and faced them. He looked beyond them, and then they all looked around. It was as if they were trapped in a snow globe, one that a small child had shaken with all his might. Snow swirled violently everywhere. They hadn't passed a tree, a boulder, or any type of landmark since they ventured away from the tunnel. Dorn had snowflakes latched to his eyelashes and Raistlin was beginning to grow icicles on his hefty beard.

"We can't make it through this," Dorn yelled. "Something isn't right."

Raistlin said something incomprehensible under the wind. They all leaned their heads in and he spoke again, "Lance's Gods are playing tricks on us."

"We have to go back to the tunnel," Dorn yelled.

Raistlin nodded as he leaned against Jared, the cold made him weaker by the minute.

192

"Okay, fine," Jared yelled. "Let's go back."

They looked around, then looked at one another.

"Which way is the tunnel?" Billy yelled.

None of them answered, and Jared and Dorn's glances met. Neither had ever seen the other with such a pained, lost look on their face.

They looked around for their footprints, but any prints in the snow had already been covered by the blizzard conditions. Billy shivered. Raistlin continued to lean on Jared. Dorn squinted his eyes and looked around. Jared's shoulders slumped, which was unusual for his character.

"We have to keep walking," Dorn said. "We will die here if we stop."

Jared nodded, "Lead the way." He looked over at Billy. Billy was shivering so badly that his shoulders shook. "Billy," Jared yelled. "Wrap an arm around Raistlin, you can share body heat."

Billy put his arm around Raistlin's waist; in return, Raistlin put his arm around Billy's shoulder and pulled his head toward him. Jared, Raistlin, and Billy walked together through what most would call the storm of the century.

Dorn led them forward. He walked in a straight path. He refused to wonder if they should be going in another direction. He knew if they started to change direction, they may do it over and over and eventually be walking in a big circle.

Soon, they were all shivering. Even Dorn's shoulders shuddered as he walked. The snow for much of the trek was just over ankle deep, but the cold was unbearable. All of them had their hands not in their pockets, but stuffed down into their pants to gain any warmth they possibly could.

They leaned forward into the wind with their eyes closed most of the time. Soon, the snow grew deeper. Thick tree trunks began to appear through the whiteout. The tops of the trees couldn't be seen. The hidden branches above them rustled with a roar that blended with the howl of the gale. More trees appeared as they walked, which lessened the power of the wind and the piercing of the snow. The tree trunks were huge; if two of the men in the group stood on each side of the tree and stretched their arms around the trunk, their fingers would barely touch. Even though the wind was less powerful within the trees, the sound was still loud. Loud enough that when Billy yelled, "Look! A cabin!" nobody heard him. But Jared and Dorn saw him raise his arm and point when he yelled. They both followed the direction of his finger; in the distance, the faint outline of a building appeared. They moved faster through the trees as the outline of the cabin grew clearer. Soon they were standing on a snowy wooden porch. Jared lifted the door latch and pushed, but the door was stuck shut. He pushed harder, then slammed his shoulder into the door. The last bit was enough to pop the door open. Once they were all inside, Jared had to slam the door shut against the fierce, blowing snow.

60

They stood in the log cabin and let their eyes adjust from the whiteout of the storm to the dim, one-roomed building that had one small window. Their heavy breathing came out in clouds in the cold cabin. A fireplace was recessed into the wall to the right of the door. A wooden table sat below the small window; there were two wooden chairs, one of them broken and lying on its side. A framed cubby in the corner was stocked full of firewood. On one shelf sat a number of folded wool blankets. Dorn pulled two of the blankets down and spread them on the floor near the fireplace.

"Raistlin," he whispered. "Lie down over here."

Raistlin shuffled to the blanket and let out a yell as he sat. He held his broken arm close to his side.

On the back wall, a bear skin with the head attached was stretched across the wall. Billy went to it and ran his hand down its fur.

Jared tossed logs into the fireplace, then he found flint stones on the dusty mantel.

Dorn saw what Jared was doing and said, "Wait, I have an idea." Dorn pulled his knife and began shaving one of the legs of the broken chair. Small strips of wood curled off the leg and fell to the floor. When he had a handful, he handed them to Jared. Jared placed them at the base of the logs and began striking the flint stones together. Sparks flew off the stones and onto the curled strips of wood.

Billy walked to the window and stood on the good chair. He reached up to a shelf above the window and began to pull cans down. They were sealed tin cans without labels or writing on them. When Billy stepped down from the chair, there were a dozen cans on the table.

"Do you think this is food?" Billy asked.

Dorn picked up one of the cans and looked at it, then he tried to turn it as if a lid would spin off. Although the wind still howled and the cabin creaked with the storm, the sound of the stones clicking together at the fireplace could be heard. Dorn pulled his knife back out and began prying at the tin can. As he began to pry the lid of the can, Jared could be heard blowing on the kindling and the smell of smoke filled the small cabin. A few seconds later, a light flickered as the fire began to take shape. Soon, the fire popped as more logs began to catch fire.

Dorn pried the lid off and smelled the contents of the can. "Soup," he said and held the can out to Jared. Jared sniffed it and nodded with approval. He set the can on the stone edge of the fireplace.

By the time the fourth can was sitting by the fire, the group had quit shivering, but the room was still cold. The walls of the cabin gave off a cold that seemed to push into the room as if a fog was trying to engulf them.

They spread out more blankets and sat near Raistlin and tried to warm themselves. Billy spotted something on the shelf above the window, and a moment later he was wiping the insides of wooden bowls with his shirt.

Soon, the cabin smelled of herbs and spices such as oregano and basil as the soup warmed. After Jared put more logs on the fire, he poured the contents of each can into a wooden bowl one at a time. He used part of a blanket as an oven mitt.

196

They began to eat the soup with wooden spoons that Billy had also found on the shelf. Raislin leaned forward and dipped his spoon into the bowl while the others held theirs in one hand and scooped with the other.

Billy, realizing the trouble Raistlin was having, set his soup by the fire, grabbed Raistlin's bowl, and held it in front of him.

"You don't have to hold my bowl for me, Billy," Raistlin said.

"That's okay, sir," Billy said. "This will warm my hands while you eat."

Raistlin took another bite and said, "This tastes just like Tessa's chicken noodle soup recipe."

Dorn paused for a moment and said, "It sure does, doesn't it?"

Jared stopped eating for a moment and said, "How is it we stumbled across a cabin in the middle of a blizzard that is fully stocked with firewood and food?"

"The Great Fathers," Raistlin said quietly.

Jared leaned his head toward Raistlin, asking him to say it again without saying a word.

Since they entered the cabin a short time before, they had spoken quietly or not at all despite the ruckus that was going on outside of the dwelling. It was as if they didn't want the storm to know they had shacked up in relief of the deadly weather.

"The Great Fathers," Raistlin said again. "The Great Fathers are helping us out, trying to help us survive and get back to Evergreen."

"Is that why this is Tessa's recipe?" Jared asked.

Raistlin nodded, "Tessa's recipe is actually my grandmother's recipe, it has been handed down. My grandfather knows it well."

"So, we are pawns of the In Between, and Lance's gods and our Great Fathers are the ones pushing us around," Dorn said as he scraped the last of his noodles out of the bottom of his bowl.

"So to speak, yes," Raistlin said.

197

After Raistlin was done eating, Billy picked up his own bowl and began eating again. Soon, they were all done eating, and the whiteout outside the cabin was growing dim. Dorn pulled a strip of bark off a log out of the bin and touched it to the fire, then he went to an oil lamp that sat on the table and lit it.

Jared took one of the empty tin cans and melted snow in it, then mixed a medicine concoction for Raistlin. They all shared one more can of soup before they snuffed the lantern and curled up to go to sleep. The winter storm still howled and the window of the cabin shook in its frame, but they were sound asleep in minutes.

Dorn woke in the middle of the night. The air in the cabin was cold, and coals glowed in the fireplace. He threw more logs onto the fire and waited for the flames to come to life again. Once the new logs took hold, he tossed more on. He covered Billy with an extra blanket, curled up in his spot, and went back to sleep.

. . .

In the morning, the first can they opened was peaches. "Have you gentlemen ever had warmed peaches?" Dorn asked.

Jared and Billy both looked at Dorn and shook their heads; Raistlin still slept on the floor.

"Well, this will be a treat then," Dorn said as he placed the can next to the fire. While the peaches cooked, Dorn mentioned that he would walk around the cabin outside and check things out.

"Look," Jared said. "Don't let the cabin get out of your sight. My dad told me some scary stories that he heard when he was a kid during the Great Blizzard of 1978." He paused for a moment while Dorn stood at the door, ready to open it. "If you lose the cabin, you might never find your way back."

Dorn thought for a moment, then said, "I understand. I won't be long."

Just minutes later, the door flew open and Dorn dumped an armload of firewood onto the floor. "There's something else," he said, then he walked back out the door and shut it behind him. Soon he was back in the cabin with an armload of frozen furs.

"Where did you get those?" Jared asked.

"They were at the bottom of a wood bin on the back side of the cabin," Dorn said.

Most of the furs were frozen together, so they set them in front of the fire to thaw.

Billy was tasked to melt snow in the left over tin cans. He topped the cans with snow over and over until the can was to the rim with water, then he let the water boil. Once cooled, he set the can aside.

Jared and Dorn spread out the furs once they thawed. There were two wolf furs, along with several rabbit, fox, and beaver furs.

Raistlin woke in pain. He held his broken arm.

Billy fed him some peaches while Jared made another one of Cambria's recipes for pain.

Jared and Dorn spoke quietly while they inventoried the firewood and the cans of food. They were trying to determine when they would run out of each. They knew the storm outside would not let up. They decided when they ran out of heat, it would be time to leave. They estimated that they could stay for three more days.

So, for the next three days, none of them left the cabin, and the storm raged on. Raistlin spent most of the time sleeping. Billy's duties were to keep a fresh supply of water. Dorn and Jared worked the furs to make clothing to wear in the storm. They worked the smaller furs so they would make wraps around their shoes and boots, and mittens for their hands. They pulled all of the lashings that were used to keep the drawings of the In Between together. They used the lashings to tie up shoe covers and to tie mittens so they could slip them over their hands.

Once they were out of leather strips, Jared took his belt off, handed it to Dorn, and said, "Here, cut this into strips."

"You sure?"

Jared nodded.

Dorn cut the buckle off the belt and then cut fine strips out of the belt with his knife. He was careful and tedious in his work. Once the belt was cut, Dorn had plenty of leather strips to continue to make the clothing.

At times, Billy recited Robert Frost poems from memory while Dorn and Jared worked on the clothing. Dorn would often take his eyes from his work and glance at Billy in admiration while Billy recited the poems. During Billy's life on Earth, he took to reading poetry after Anna died; it was something to help him deal with the solitude of losing a spouse.

They worked until light no longer came through the window. They snuffed out the oil lamp in order to save fuel. Billy had fresh water in every can available, then he heated up three more cans of food. One of the cans was clam chowder, and Dorn made a horrible face when he tasted it. Regardless, he went on eating it.

Jared tossed more logs into the fireplace, then they covered up in blankets and the furs they had been working with and were lulled to sleep with the sounds of the creaking cabin, the rattling window, and the light snore of Raistlin, who had already been sleeping for hours.

The next morning they rationed out their food so it would last for one more day. They checked the fire bin with satisfaction. Dorn and Jared continued to work on the furs. They began to incorporate the blankets as liners for the new clothing.

Billy began to do a dress rehearsal for his new garb. He tightened his new furry boots with a double blanketed liner. A wolf pelt fell over his shoulders like a trench coat, but what topped off the new outfit was the head covering that Jared had walked over and placed on Billy's head. Just a bit earlier, Dorn had cut the head off the bear skin rug that was stretched across the wall. He did it so Raistlin could drape the bearskin over himself when they decided to venture back out into the blizzard. The head of the bear, with the lower jaw already removed, sat on Billy's head perfectly. They lined the inside of the bear's head with a layer of blankets for a softer fit. When Jared placed it on Billy's head, the extra skin around the neck of the bear fell down to Billy's shoulders. Billy looked at the others, raised his hands in the air, opened his mouth wide, and showed his teeth.

"Aaar!" he yelled.

Dorn and Jared laughed. Raistlin smiled, leaning against the wall and drinking his warm medicine.

Billy smiled at their reactions and walked about the small cabin, finally stopping and gazing out the window at the horrid conditions that continued outside. He looked like a small mountain man in his authentic clothing. The bear's head sat upon his head with the snout poking out like the brim of a baseball cap. The fangs of the bear poked down just inches from Billy's eyes. He remembered seeing kids with Davy Crockett coonskin caps on television shows when he was in his world, but nobody had ever worn a bear skull for a cap. He continued to look down at his furry outfit and walk around. He caught a glimpse of his shadow from the fireplace and turned his head so he could see the silhouette of the bear's head on the wall. He threw his arms in the air and stepped forward, then he laughed at the shadow he saw. He stepped forward again but tripped and fell to the wooden floor. He laughed again as he rose to his feet. His outfit was dusty on the elbows and knees from the fall, but Billy was none the worse for wear.

Dorn leaned over from where he sat and looked at what caused Billy to fall. Two boards butted into one another on the floor, one a bit higher than the other. Like any other cabin with a wood floor, there were wood planks, row after row, and in spots they butted together. The butt joints were always scattered for strength, and in a small cabin like this one, there may be only one butt joint per row, if any at all. But this row had two butt joints, both near the center of the room. In between the butt joints, there was a board about twice the length of Billy's foot.

Dorn scooted himself over to the short board and fingered the joint. He pulled his knife and began to pry at it. Jared stopped his work and Raistlin lost his blank gaze and looked to see what was happening.

Nails squeaked as Dorn pried at the board; slowly it began to come up. Once he could get his fingers under it, he gave it a strong tug. With a loud squeak, the board was standing at a right angle from the floor. He peeked into the rectangular void in the floor, then held his head at an angle to see farther under the board. He reached into the hole and pulled out a brass colored cylinder. He held it before him and pulled on it. It doubled in length. It was a spyglass. Dorn wiped the ends, held it to one eye, and looked out into the storm.

After a moment, he pulled it down and said, "I suppose The Great Fathers thought we might need this." He set the spyglass on the floor and reached back inside the hole. This time he pulled out a flat disc. He leaned back into a more comfortable position and turned the object over in his hands.

"It looks like a compass," Jared said.

Dorn turned it over one more time, then handed it to Jared. Jared held it in his hand, then turned it with the other like an old-fashioned radio dial. "I've never seen a compass like this, though." He said.

He handed it to Billy. Billy also held the compass flat in his hand. On the end of the needle of the compass, it was shaped like a semicircle. He turned himself around as he held the object flat, the needle floating inside the glass top. No matter where he turned, the semicircle end of the needle kept pointing toward the corner on the left side of the fireplace. The outer circle of the compass consisted of three rows of dials, one inside the other. Billy turned the outer dial.

It didn't move freely; the compass was aged. He turned the next dial, then the one inside the other two. Each of the three dials had graduations on them, a few of them bolder and longer than the others.

"I never learned about this one in Boy Scouts," Billy said as he handed the complicated mechanism back to Jared.

...

When Dorn and Jared finished the furs, the white storm was nothing but black again with nightfall. They threw more logs on, and Billy warmed three more cans of food. Dorn and Jared set the compass on the floor between them. They sat cross-legged and looked at the contraption. Each of them took turns holding it to see it up close. They turned the dials to all different points in an attempt to understand how it worked. It was obvious that the needle kept pointing to one thing, which Jared assumed was magnetic north. How the graduated lines worked with each other, Jared had no idea. A normal compass he could navigate in his sleep. He'd learned about them at a young age. Whether he knew the trail he was hiking or not, he always used one. This one was complicated. Both men were lost in concentration on the compass when Billy said the food was ready.

Billy helped Raistlin eat his food since he could still barely lift his arm. Raistlin waved him off after half the can was gone. Raistlin snuggled into his blankets, and Billy adjusted them until Raistlin was comfortable. He scooted to the other two and finished the can of food.

When Dorn and Jared finished, Dorn said, "Billy."

Billy looked at him.

"We need to clean those cans," Dorn nodded to the ones they had just finished. "Then we need to stuff them with snow. I'll help you."

They rounded up the cans and set them by the door. Dorn put on all of his new clothing. His legs were covered with wolf fur, his foot coverings made from beaver pelts. He slipped a moose skin over his head and slid his upper limbs through the arm holes like he was donning a poncho. He placed a fur cap on his head and threw a strip of blanket around his neck for a scarf.

Billy still wore his new garb that he had dressed in earlier. He also had a blanket for a scarf, then he placed the bear head cap on his head.

"Ready?" Dorn said.

"Ready!" Billy said.

They opened the door and tossed the cans outside, then they slipped out the door and pulled it shut. The wind swirled and blew snow off the roof, so it seemed to Billy and Dorn that the snow was coming from everywhere. They grabbed handfuls of snow with their rabbit fur mittens and cleaned the cans. Then they began to stuff the tin cans with snow, packing it in as tight as they could.

"Keep packing the snow, Billy," Dorn yelled over the wind. He began to walk away with the compass held up in his hand. He tilted the compass to where he could see it from the glow of the fire through the cabin window. He walked out far enough to still be able to see the small structure. He slipped the compass back into his pocket and walked back to the cabin. He and Billy stuffed snow into all of the cans, and then went inside and placed them in front of the fire.

61

After eating the last of the warm food the following morning, they drank what water was left since there was no convenient container to carry it with. Dorn stood by the window and explained his theory on how the compass worked.

"I believe there will be an obstacle of some sort, maybe a mountain or a lake," He said to Jared. "If we line up these graduations," he turned the two inside dials so the upper graduations were in line with each other. "Then there is a darker one here, and another dark one here," he pointed to each darker line with his thumbnails. Dorn's dark eyes glanced at Jared for a moment, then back at the compass. "We keep the needle in the center of the two dark lines and follow it as far as we can, we will eventually walk to whatever the obstacle is. Then we follow either the dark line on the left or the one on the right."

"How will we know which one?" Jared asked.

"We will have to decide when we get there. We will have to pay close attention to the graduations as we follow the dark one. We have to hold the compass steady so we don't lose our direction." Dorn rubbed his short, dark beard for a moment, then continued, "Since we think the needle is always pointing toward the arches we need to reach, as we walk in the direction the dark lines are pointing, the needle will slowly change direction on the compass as it follows where the arches are. Once the needle reaches the other dark line, we change direction and walk in the direction of the other dark line. When we do this, the needle will drift back the other way. Once it reaches dead center again, then we follow the needle again."

"What if it doesn't work?" Billy asked as he looked at the compass.

Dorn shrugged, "It is our only hope to navigate through this storm." He slipped the compass into his pocket and looked out the window. "We could get lost forever."

. . .

They helped Raistlin to his feet and helped him dress into his custom winter gear. He held his arm tight to his side as they prepared to walk out the door. Each of them had cattail stalks in their pockets. They saved the bland food since they were able to eat warm food for the past two and a half days. They stood, all facing each other. Their scarves, cut from the blankets, were wrapped tight around their necks. Billy had his bear's head for a cap. Raistlin had part of a deer hide on his head held tight with a leather strap. Dorn and Jared each had a cap that consisted of a portion of a blanket hung over their head with a strip of cloth holding it in place.

"Are we ready?" Jared asked.

"As ready as we'll ever be," Raistlin said. He looked as though he didn't have enough energy to make it out the door, let alone make a hike through the blizzard of the century.

They all nodded and walked out the door, one by one. Dorn checked the compass, then he led the way through the blowing snow.

With their new winter weather gear, walking through the storm was much more bearable than it was before they had reached the cabin. Dorn and

206

Jared pulled their hats down low enough over their eyes that they could barely see. Billy cupped his hands around his eyes to block the piercing snow. Raistlin held onto Billy's new coat as they walked, and he kept his eyes closed most of the time. Dorn checked the compass often, sometimes changing their course in a subtle way.

Trees appeared in the white storm from time to time, but they did not weaken the brutal wind. Even with their winter clothing, they all began to shiver. They gathered in a group hug and patted each other on the back to try to warm up, then they continued walking. They walked into the night. There was no relief from the wind and snow and nothing to use for firewood, so they kept walking.

By the middle of the night, when the temperatures were at their lowest, they were doing whatever they could to stay warm. The others beat their hands against their thighs and jumped up and down to get warm, but Raistlin's weak condition limited him. The others gathered around and tried to warm him.

Once the sky lightened, the temperature rose several degrees which seemed like a relief to them, although the air was still frigidly cold. As they walked, the sun seemed to appear more through the storm. As a hazy glowing ball in the storm, it was directly in front of them as they followed the direction of the needle. The wind seemed to die down and the snow thinned out, bringing more sunlight to the travelers.

Dorn stopped walking and held his arms out for the others to stop. He walked forward a few more steps. "Step to me, gentlemen."

The others stepped forward. With each step, the snow thinned more. They stopped where the snow on the ground stopped. They stood at the top of a cliff. Where the ground ended, the storm seemed to end as well. The snow swirled around them and disappeared as it flew over the cliff. The sun illuminated the valley that sat several hundred feet below them. There was no snow on the floor of the valley, which consisted of forests, small grassy plains, and a river that made small curves through the landscape. The river eventually dumped into a lake that was shaped like a boot.

They stood at the edge of the storm. Anything that blew beyond the edge of the cliff seemed to melt in mid-air.

Dorn pulled the compass from his pocket and looked at it. He looked up at the sun, then back down to the compass.

"We head that way," he pointed to the left.

They walked in the direction he pointed. On the right side of them, a sunny valley sat with cliff walls that surrounded a third of the horizon. On the other side of them, the winter storm continued its eternal blast.

They lifted their caps to see better as they walked. They constantly looked to their right at the valley below. Soon, the terrain changed as a path began to lead down and a cliff wall grew to the left. They walked down this path which was no wider than one of them could spread their arms. The snow disappeared as they reached the lower elevations. They continued down the path, a sheer wall that went up on one side, a sheer drop on the other. The path never narrowed, so they walked with no worries. The path followed the sheer wall with a slight curve. By the time the path leveled out onto the valley, Dorn and Jared had removed their head coverings. The air was cool, but the sun brought a natural warmth they hadn't felt in days.

They stood at the base of the path and looked around. Beautiful trees and green plains scattered the land before them. Several hundred feet above them, the winter storm still dealt its anger. Snow squalls swirled over the edge of the cliff and its flakes melted in thin air.

Dorn pulled out the spyglass and extended it. He held it to his right eye and slowly scanned the area. He pulled it away from his eye and continued to gaze into the distance. He held it to his side and handed it to Jared.

Jared took it and looked through it. Not satisfied with anything he saw; he collapsed it and slid it into his own pocket.

Dorn pulled the compass and adjusted it to the direction of the sun. He double checked his bearings then pointed and said, "We have to go this way."

Realizing that Raistlin was on the verge of exhaustion, they decided to stop. They rested against the sheer rock wall and let the sun beat on them. They slid their fur shoe coverings off their feet. Raistlin fidgeted with his head covering, then Billy helped him remove it. They munched on the last of the cattail stalks.

Billy stood and pulled two tin cans from inside his clothing. He had grabbed them at the last moment before they left the cabin, just in case. "I hear a waterfall," he said. "I should try to get some water."

"I'll go with you, Billy," Dorn said and stood.

When they began to walk away, Jared said, "Hey." He grabbed the compass that Dorn had set on the ground just a bit ago. He handed it to Dorn and said, "Don't get lost."

Dorn took the compass and held it up, "As Jared Collins would say, 'even the best hikers use a compass.'"

Jared leaned his head back and felt the warmth of the sun as he closed his eyes. Raistlin did the same and soon began to snore.

Dorn and Billy came back with two tin cans full of water. "Drink," Dorn said. "This is as fresh as it gets. Straight from a mountain stream." They woke Raistlin, passed the tin cans around, and drank the cool water.

When the water was gone, they were back on their feet. They followed a needle on an ancient compass with hopes it would take them home.

. . .

Dorn's theory on the compass was proving to be correct. When they began to follow the needle after their afternoon rest, the needle began to drift back toward the center of the graduations. Their path took them along the edge of the boot-shaped lake. Dorn had predicted that they would encounter an obstacle or two, and this had to be one of them.

Once they were clear of the lake, the needle of the compass was in the center of the graduation lines. They changed their course, followed the path of the needle, and walked toward the sunset.

62

Raistlin sat back against a tree trunk and gazed at the semicircle of arches. Time after time, when they reached the tunnels to other places, the structure that housed them always looked the same. The words above the arches were what was different. New places to go every time.

Dorn and Jared picked raspberries and strawberries from a wild patch under the light of a full moon.

Billy consoled a girl who was weeping in front of one of the arches. She was lost and had no idea how to get back home. Billy spoke with her for a while, then went back and retrieved the maps from Dorn. He laid them out on the ground, and he and the girl looked over the maps. Billy tried to jog her memory with the names of some of the arches to see if any would ring a bell. On the third page of the maps, she pointed to a labeled arch.

"Are you sure?"

She nodded, and the tears on her face began to evaporate.

"Okay, try to remember the tunnels you will take from here," Billy said. "If you get lost, just try to backtrack and we can look at the maps again."

They looked over the maps one more time under the moonlight and munched on the fruit that was picked.

The girl nodded and trotted off. Just before she disappeared into a tunnel, she turned and yelled, "Thank you!"

Billy smiled and waved.

Still in his furs, Raistlin was curled up on the ground, sound asleep. The others laid their clothing out like sleeping bags. They sat on them as they looked over the drawings.

Small clouds came in and blocked the moonlight, making it too difficult to read the maps any longer. The remaining three curled up and went to sleep.

. . .

When they woke, the arches were gone. The tree that Raistlin had slept near was gone as well. Dorn and Jared leaned up and looked around.

Billy stood and stretched, then said, "Holy Toledo, what happened?"

"Lance's gods have done it again."

The three of them looked over at Raistlin. None of them knew he was awake.

"They are doing everything they can to keep us from Evergreen," Raistlin said. "We should have never gone to sleep. Who knows where we are now, with no arches to guide us."

The sound of small waves rolling into a shoreline filled the morning air. Behind them was a vast sea, there was no sign of land on the other side. A big wooden boat with a tall mast floated on the water a few stone's throws away from the shore. The tall mast on the boat swayed back and forth. The small ripples from the waves reflected the morning sunlight.

Billy placed his bear cap on his head to help block the sun. They gathered their furs and walked to the shore. They knew what they had to do.

A small wooden raft sat in the sand. They pushed it into the water and hopped on. With their momentum and a few paddles with their hands, they reached the wooden boat. They tossed their furs into the boat and helped Raistlin climb over the side. The rest of them followed, and the small wooden raft was left to float away.

The boat was magnificent. Billy walked around the small deck in awe. It was an old Viking boat. The bow curled up into a dragon's head, its face frozen in a permanent snarl. Like the bow, the stern was also carved from wood that formed the tail of the dragon. Scale after scale had been carved along the dragon's tail.

A sail was folded at length on the base of the mast. Long wooden oars hung on the inside of both sides of the boat. Wooden seats adorned the bow, stern, port, and starboard sides of the ship. They were molded and finished as if a carpenter had meticulously put the final touches on a fireplace mantle. The maritime vessel was exquisite.

While the other three ran their hands along the trim on the ship and took in its beauty, Raistlin rested on the sole against the seat at the stern. "Fair winds and following seas, my friends," he said. "Fair winds and following seas." Then he leaned his head to the side and rested.

Dorn and Jared were worried about him but said nothing. There was nothing to do until they reached either somewhere where there was help or Evergreen. None of them had any idea when, or if, they would reach Evergreen.

Dorn pulled the rope from the port side, lifted the anchor, and set it on the wooden sole. Jared took one of the oars, dipped it in the water, and pulled it to his side so the ship would point to the opening sea. They messed with the ropes that were tied to the sail and the mast. Once they figured it out, the sail was up to the top of the mast, and the boat headed out to sea.

Dorn pulled the compass from his pocket and looked at it. There was nothing fancy this time; they just had to follow the needle. No obstacle in sight.

Soon, the land they had just left was a thin streak on the horizon, yet there was still nothing to view but the sea ahead of them. The boat sped along with the wind; warm sea water splashed at them when the bow struck a wave just right. Dorn pulled his spyglass and looked over the horizon. The movement of the boat and the repetition of the bow crashing into the waves were mesmerizing. They all fell into their own thoughts as the Viking boat cruised along.

There is something special that being out at sea can do to a person. The tranquil sounds and the endless waves can calm even those with the shortest attention spans. Although Raistlin slept due to his weakened condition, the others sat wide awake as the boat cut through wave after wave.

Every time the bow hit a wave, Billy would hear a rattle under his seat. He got up and kneeled to try to hear better. When it happened again, he pulled on one of the boards under his seat. The board slid to the side, revealing a small storage compartment. He pulled out two spears that were as long as his arm span; a length of rope was attached to each spear.

Dorn and Jared had been watching while Billy pulled the weapons from the compartment.

"You think we'll do some fishing?" Billy asked as he held out the spears.

Dorn nodded and said, "It looks like The Great Fathers are watching over us once again."

They sailed into the sunset. They decided that the wind was too much of a commodity to drop the sails and sleep, so Jared curled up in his furs, and Dorn took the first shift of sailing through the night.

Billy stayed awake as Dorn checked the compass from time to time and adjusted the sail accordingly. Billy lay back and looked at the stars that filled the sky from one end of the horizon to the other. He felt as though he was in an observatory; he had never seen so many stars so bright.

Billy looked at Dorn and realized Dorn was looking up into the sky as well. "In my world, there are some places where you can see more stars than in other places," Billy said. "Like in the desert or out at sea. In some places, they say you can even see the Milky Way. But, in Corktown, there were always too many city lights to see all of those stars."

"What's the Milky Way, Billy?" Dorn asked as he got more comfortable in his seat.

"It's the galaxy that my world is in. Kind of like my planet's home," Billy said. "It is spread out like a spiral, and it has several legs. We are in one of the legs, and sometimes you can see the other legs at night."

"Can you see the Milky Way tonight, Billy?" Dorn asked.

"I don't think so. But, I've never seen it. Only heard about it."

Soon, Billy was asleep, and Dorn spent half of the night sailing the boat in solitude. When he and Jared switched shifts, the wind had died considerably.

When morning came, their stomachs growled. They ate a bit of the wild fruit they had gathered before the voyage and left some for Raistlin. Dorn found one of the tins and dipped it in the sea and brought it to his mouth for a drink.

Before he drank a drop, Jared said, "Dorn! Don't!"

Dorn stopped and looked at him with a questioning stare.

"You can't drink that," Jared said.

"Why?"

"It's sea water, it's full of salt," Jared said and thought for a moment. "Taste it."

Dorn dipped a finger into the tin can, pulled it out, and tasted it.

"It's salty," Jared said. "Like how you cure your meat after you hunt."

Dorn nodded.

"You can't have too much of it. The sea water is salt water, it can kill you."

Dorn looked down at the can, then tossed the water back to the sea. He dropped the can to the ground and said, "So, what do we do for water?"

Jared and Billy had no answer as they both looked at the cloudless sky. Raistlin snoozed at the rear of the boat.

The sea flattened as the wind died enough to make the sail slack on the mast. By the middle of the day, they were afloat on a flat sea.

By this time, Raistlin was awake, eating some of the fruit the others had saved for him. "A flat sea and a sky with no clouds," he said. "No water to drink and I am eating food my friends are starving for at the moment. It looks like Lance's gods are playing their part in this wicked game." He held a handful of berries out to the others, but they all declined, as he knew they would.

. . .

Jared straddled the side of the boat, spear in hand, while Dorn stood on the bow seat and looked through the spyglass. Soon, they both realized their efforts were futile. They sat down on their seats in defeat. They stayed in their respective places on the boat for the next two days with no food or water. The temperature was warm enough that they didn't need their furs, and even during the midday sun, the heat was never overwhelming. Regardless, the dehydration began to take its toll. They all draped themselves in their spots on the boat. They were all suffering, but Raistlin was dying. The rest of them knew that fact. They also knew they were helpless with the lack of resources at hand.

Another day passed, and then clouds began to fill the sky. By midday, rain began to fall. Dorn and Jared stretched one of the furs between them after cutting a hole in the middle of it. The rainwater ran down the fur into the hole like a funnel. Billy placed one of the tin cans below the hole for collection.

Raistlin was the first to drink, then the others took their turn. It rained harder, and soon they all had their fill of water.

The clouds darkened, and thunder rumbled in the distance. An occasional jagged bolt of lightning flashed across the sky.

Jared focused his attention on the sea after something had caught his eye. He stood up and grabbed one of the spears. The others looked at what Jared was looking at. Fish were jumping. As far as they could see, fish broke the surface of the water and then smacked back down with a splash. Some of the fish were small, yet some were half the size of their boat. Jared leaned against the side of the boat with a spear in hand. He watched a few of the close fish jump, estimating when he would have to release his spear. He released his spear as soon as a medium-sized fish broke the water in front of them. His timing of the launch was perfect, but his aim was not. His spear flew higher than the fish. Jared pulled the spear back to the boat with the rope. His second attempt was a little closer. His third was spot on as the spearhead poked through the fish. He pulled the spear back to the boat with the fish on the end of it. He pulled it off the spear and readied himself for another throw.

Jared tried to spear another while Dorn cut open the caught fish, gutted it, and scraped the scales off it with his knife. He sliced the meat and handed the pieces out. Jared tossed another fish onto the wooden floorboards and sat down with the rest of them. Billy hesitated while the others took a bite of the raw protein. Dorn looked at Billy and nodded. Billy took a bite of the silky piece and was surprised at the taste. He didn't care for the texture, but the flavor juices burst in his mouth.

Once they had their fill, they tossed the uneaten pieces of the fish and its guts back out to sea. The dark clouds had moved in closer and the waves were beginning to form white caps. The boat began to rock in the waves and they were once again sailing.

Soon they had to lower the sail because the wind was too blustery. Regardless, the boat still moved at a good pace. They steered it with a small rudder off the back. The rain beat down on them and the waves began to crash over the sides of the boat. The seawater washed across the sole and through the scuppers, back out to sea. Lightning flashed directly above them and thunder mixed in with the roar of the wind and waves. The waves hit the boat hard enough to toss the crew from one side of the boat to another. Dorn grabbed one of the ropes and tied it around Billy's waist, then he tied the other end to the base of the mast.

The gloomy, gray skies turned to complete darkness once night approached. Every few seconds lightning flashed, allowing them to guide their way. Dorn worked the rudder as Jared navigated from the front of the boat. Billy hugged the base of the mast with his eyes closed. Raistlin showed more clarity with the escalation of the storm. He sat on the sole and held onto the bench next to him as the boat rocked. Jared yelled commands back to Dorn which were seldom heard over the wind. The biggest waves knocked them from their spots on the boat. How none of them were tossed into the sea and lost forever is a pure miracle. The Great Fathers were looking out for them once again.

In the wee hours of the morning, the storm finally calmed. The boat drifted aimlessly as its occupants fell asleep, decimated with exhaustion.

63

Jared was the first to wake. The sun was shining and birds were chirping. The boat was tilted to one side. Jared tapped Dorn's shoulder to wake him. Dorn stirred and rubbed his eyes, once he realized the boat was tilted he sprung to his knees. They were beached. The boat had drifted while they slept and ran aground on an island.

"Billy, wake up," Jared said as he and Dorn stepped out of the boat. They stood in the sand and took in the situation. The beach ran off in the distance on each side of them. Before them, the sand continued up a small hill and then turned to grass. After the grass was a thick forest. Birds of all types were heard. Jared leaned forward for a moment, sure he had heard a primate of some sort.

Billy walked and stood between them. "Where the heck are we? Africa?" he said.

Jared put his hand on Billy's shoulder, "I'm guessing there is an arch somewhere on the other side of this world that says just that. Africa."

Dorn pulled the compass from his pocket and held it so Jared could see. The needle pointed to the forest.

"Well?" Jared said.

Dorn looked back at Raistlin. "Let's wake the old man. We'll bring those spears as well."

"Got it," Jared said.

They left the boat behind, the eyes of the dragon watching them go.

The first several steps into the forest consisted of thick brush and tree branches. Once they were past the thickness on the outskirts of the forest, the trees and brush seemed to thin. There was no trail to follow, they just dodged the trees as they walked. The needle of the compass told them the direction to follow. They walked in a single file line. Dorn led the way with his compass in hand. Billy followed him with Raistlin behind and Jared taking up the back.

As they walked, the sounds of the macaws, toucans, and parrots filled the forest. The humidity and temperature were high enough to make each of them sweat as they walked at their casual pace. Monkeys and baboons were heard as they hiked. Another hour later, they saw the hairy mammals in the trees. The primates watched their more intelligent counterparts navigate across the forest floor.

Often, the group stopped to rest due to Raistlin's condition. They were grateful that he was still able to walk.

They ventured on and encountered a small stream and followed it. They followed it until it dropped off a ledge. They stood at the top of the ledge and looked down. The waterfall spilled into a pool of water several hundred feet below. Surrounding the pool of water was a series of arches, one after the other, forming a semicircle.

They noticed a set of stone stairs that zig-zagged down the side of the rock wall and began to descend them. The ancient steps were tricky to navigate. They were slimy with moss, and the height of each step varied as they descended. There was no handrail to hold onto; one slip and they would go tumbling down the steps. Raistlin draped his good arm around Dorn and held the broken one at his side as they carefully took each step. Jared walked in front of them, sometimes walking backward with his hands held out in case Raistlin happened to trip. Once they were at the bottom of the stairs, they stood before the arches that seemed enormous despite the cliffs behind them.

Every stop before the arches became routine: they ate what food they had or could find nearby, and they studied the maps. The maps didn't blatantly show them where Evergreen was, but their intuition led them. On one of the drawings, one of the arches led to nowhere. All of the other ones were intricately tied together. Page after page, the mapping of the tunnels could have confused even the most experienced cartographer, but the group seemed to understand the stack of drawings. They spoke and pointed to different arches and expressed their opinions on where to go next. Billy, who hardly remembered drawing the maps, navigated them as if he had drawn them up only a week before.

Once again, by the time they drew up a plan, it was getting dark. Raistlin's poor condition forced them to rest for the night. Despite the sounds of baboons in the distance, they all eventually fell asleep.

This time the arches were still there when they woke. They stretched and drank water from a nearby stream. Soon, they walked through another arch.

They stood in a mountain range. A trail cut across the face of the mountain, a switchback visible in the distance. Jagged mountains lined the horizon, most of them were capped with snow. The group slipped on their furs to fight the nip in the air. Billy's bear cap remained on his head as it had for several days. They walked the skinny trail, which was an obstacle course of rocks and tree roots.

The bear's nose turned toward the opposing mountain range, and Billy pointed. "Look at those birds!" He spoke. "They look huge!"

The others looked, except for Raistlin. Three big, gray-colored birds flew in slow circles in the open air above the valley.

"Those things gotta be huge up close," Billy said. "What kind are they?"

"Too far away to tell, Billy," Jared said. "They are big, though."

221

They turned their focus back on the trail, which seemed like a disaster waiting to happen with Raistlin's condition. He walked like a zombie, unresponsive except for commands on where to step or which way to turn.

Jared had difficulties breathing in the thin air. Before they left Evergreen, he had been exercising to try to strengthen from his diminished lung capacity, but he often became winded in certain situations.

The sky was bright and brought a little warmth to them in the brisk breeze. Soon, clouds rolled in below them. White mists swirled around the mountainside and trees and wisped around the branches and rocks. The sun continued to shine on them as they descended down into the new blanket of clouds. Once they reached the mist they stopped. Before them was a sea of white. It looked as though they could swim, or even walk, to the mountains on the other side. Instead, they continued down the trail and were engulfed in fog.

The white mist only allowed them to see the trees around them, but not beyond. They followed the trail in a single file line. Jared held on to the back of Raistlin's fur coat to steady him as he walked.

The white mist that began to swirl around them was soon gone, replaced by icy snowflakes flying horizontally. The wind raced to a howling velocity, causing travel to be impossible with the piercing snowflakes. They hunkered down near a large tree trunk and covered themselves with the furs. They were caught in a sudden mountain storm.

Jared had read about these storms that catch hikers off guard and can often be deadly. "Gather in tight," he yelled over the wind. "This could get worse! Raistlin and Billy! Get between us! Cover up with all the furs we have!"

They all curled up together with their arms wrapped around one another. Under their cover, it was complete darkness, while outside was a squall that was a total whiteout.

An hour passed, then another. The furs and body heat kept them warm enough to keep them from shivering. When the storm passed, they crawled from beneath the furs to a clear sky above them. They regained their bearings and continued to move along. The switchbacks led them out of the trees to an open view of the valley below. The trail led to the right as a narrow ledge on the side of a mountain. The slope below them disappeared into a shroud of mist hundreds of feet below. Ahead of them, the trail led to a bridge that was suspended across the valley. The bridge was hundreds of feet long and sagged into a slight smile as it connected mountain to mountain. Three of the large birds they had seen earlier circled above the bridge.

"Jared," Billy said. "Those birds look like that one that tried to take you when we were in t he Dark Forest."

Jared absently rubbed one of his shoulders and nodded.

The bridge grew closer and the birds became more vivid. They looked like pterodactyls from the dinosaur age, similar to the birds in   the Dark Forest. The birds continued to circle over the bridge, waiting for someone to walk across.

The four travelers stood at the start of the bridge. It consisted of four ropes strung over the valley to the other side. Two of the ropes were handholds. Pine planks spanned the gap between the lower ropes, making a sketchy walkway. Some of the planks were broken and hanging; their splintered ends pointing to the valley below. Often there were gaps between the boards, like keys missing from an antique piano. The light breeze that carried through the mountains caused the rope bridge to sway; the boards that touched each other responded with squeaks that sang in unison with the gale.

The group stood only a few feet away from where the ropes were anchored to the rugged ground. The birds circled.

"Oh,   jeepers," Billy said. "I don't like heights."

"You'll be fine, Billy," Raistlin groaned. "You are a courageous young man. If it wasn't for you and those maps you drew, we may not have made it this far."

223

Billy sucked in a deep breath and slowly let it out.

"Just follow my steps, Billy," Dorn said. "Raistlin and Jared will follow you."

Dorn stepped on the first plank of the bridge, then the second; his weight at the start of the bridge didn't affect the results of the wind buffeting the span in the center. The prehistoric birds continued to circle overhead.

Billy followed Dorn's every step, and Jared watched Raistlin's every move. Raistlin's steps were ginger and slow, and he often misstepped for a second and grabbed a tighter hold of the ropes.

The oversized birds began to swoop down at them. Their wings whooshed above their heads. Jared ducked as one of the birds tried to grab him with its claws. The bridge swayed with the shifts in weight as each of them avoided the creatures. They all held on to the handholds tighter and stopped walking. Once the bridge became still, they began to walk again. The birds continued their assault on the group. One bird swooped down and struck Billy with its wing. Billy stumbled and grabbed one of the handholds with both hands. Another bird attacked seconds later and grabbed Billy, lifting him off the planks for a moment.

Billy screamed and waved his arms and kicked his legs. He squirmed under the bird's grasp and the animal dropped him. Billy landed on the planks, but his momentum slid him to the edge. He tried to grip the plank but slipped off the walkway. He was able to grab one of the ropes that held the planks in place.

At the same moment that Billy slipped off the walkway, Jared lurched forward and yelled, "Billy!" as he tried to reach around Raistlin, who held on for dear life himself.

Billy swung back and forth under the bridge while Jared tried to reach him.

As Billy hung from the span, Dorn turned to help. The birds dove in from above and disrupted any efforts to reach Billy.

A moment later Billy's hand slipped from the rope and he fell toward the valley below. At first, he pumped his arms in a backward circle as if he were about to fall off a cliff. He soon stopped and slowly tumbled through the air. His bear skull cap never left his head as he vanished into the mist.

The birds raced to follow him and soon disappeared. Jared lay on the walkway, his arm extended downward in between broken planks as he watched the mist swirl where Billy had just fallen through. The only sounds were the light breeze blowing between the mountains and the creak of the bridge. He whispered Billy's name over and over.

Dorn squatted and looked at the planks at his feet, unable to speak.

Raistlin stayed standing. His eyes were closed as he held onto a rope with his good arm.

They began to walk again, now walking up the rope bridge as they neared the other side. When he stepped off the last plank onto the rugged terrain, Jared kneeled on the ground, tilted his head to the sky, and screamed. He leaned forward and punched the damp ground over and over. He yelled and cursed, screaming Billy's name, then his brother's name. Tears rolled down his cheeks as his anger welled.

Dorn stood in his stoic fashion, but his eyes were ice cold as he gazed over the valley. He clenched his teeth, and his breath came out in a fog in the cold air.

Raistlin leaned down to Jared and put a hand on his shoulder. His long gray hair fell onto his face. "He is gone," Raistlin said. "I am probably next. You and Dorn must make it back to Evergreen." His hand patted Jared's shoulder, "We must move on."

64

Although thoughts raced through their minds, they were silent as they continued their hike. The trail they walked snaked around the side of the mountain. The trees had gotten taller as they descended to the lower elevations.

As dusk began to settle in, heavy snow began to fall. It piled on their shoulders and dampened their hair.

Dorn held his hand out for a moment then pointed to a spot in the trees. He waved to the other two and they followed him as he left the trail. He found a small cave tucked away behind a few trees. The entrance was small, so he kneeled down and peeked inside. He looked back and nodded at Jared, then crawled into the cave.

They were able to stand, and once they were all in they let their eyes adjust to the darkness. At the back of the cave, a light flickered. Dorn walked to it, then said, "This way."

They ducked through another entrance and stepped down a few steps into a much bigger area. Lazy flames danced out of sconces that adorned the stone walls. The flames lit the entire cave. The ceiling was several dozen feet in the air, and the stalactites that hung from it created jumpy shadows as if it were a live mural. A small pool sat in the center and water dripped into it from the ceiling.

On the far wall sat a series of arches, one row on the bottom level, then another above it. The arches were just like all of the others, but these held an air of mystery due to the dancing shadows.

They sat against the wall under a sconce and looked at their maps. They sat for many minutes and spoke only a few words as they studied. Soon, the warmth of the flame above them and the exhaustion of the hike through the mountains caused them to doze off. The maps lay sprawled on Dorn's lap.

They woke hours later. The flames on the walls still flickered, and the sound of the dripping water echoed through the large cave. Soon, Dorn and Jared were helping Raistlin to his feet.

As they entered the arch, Dorn said, "Evergreen can't be far."

...

When they came out the other side, they immediately pulled their furs off. The sun was directly above and beating down. There wasn't a cloud in sight. There were cactuses scattered throughout the landscape and sand covered the mountains in the distance. Once Jared realized how much heat the sun was bringing, he tossed his fur back over his head and turned to Dorn, "These will protect us. This heat is brutal."

Dorn nodded and began cutting the furs into pieces that worked as over-the-head ponchos. Once they had their heads and shoulders covered, they left the remainder of the furs behind and walked into the hot desert.

After a few hours, they were moving much slower, their mouths were dry, and their legs were weak. Raistlin could barely stand. Walking was a miracle at that point.

Although they had been following the direction that the compass pointed, Dorn pointed in the ten o'clock direction at a column of rocks that jutted out of the ground. They changed direction and soon found themselves sitting in the shade.

"We can't walk in this," Dorn said. He squinted as he gazed into the distance. The crow's feet around his dark eyes were dry and wrinkled from the arid heat. "We have to wait here. Maybe we can walk when the sun goes down."

"I guess we should have thought of that earlier," Jared said as he lay down on the gritty surface.

"We didn't know it would be this bad," Dorn said.

"Are you sure this is the right way to go?" Jared asked as he stared up into the sky with his hand behind his head.

"We chose the correct tunnel," Raistlin said from a sitting position. "I looked at the maps when you both did. You made the right decision." His voice was hoarse and dry. His gray hair looked thin and unhealthy. His skin sagged from his arms, and his lips were cracked.

With no food and no water, there was nothing to do but wait. Raistlin dozed off, but Dorn and Jared just rested with their eyes closed. The heat was too unbearable to hold a conversation.

Later that day when the sun went down, the air cooled. Once stars began to glow in the sky, they stood up and moved on. They walked through the night. All of them moved at a snail's pace. The stars and the moon lit the surroundings enough to keep their bearings. Dorn checked the compass often.

Although they walked through the night in cool air and no sunshine, the dry air still took its toll on the three of them. When the sun broke over the horizon, they walked toward a small knoll in the desert in hopes of finding shade.

Jared stopped walking and pointed to the sky to his left. He tried to speak, but nothing came out. He swallowed with pain and tried again. "Birds."

Dorn looked in the direction Jared pointed. Raistlin's arm was draped around Dorn's shoulder, and Dorn had an arm wrapped around Raistlin's waist. Raistlin was leaning on him like a person who was too inebriated to stand. In the distance, a handful of birds circled in the sky. From where they stood, they just looked like specks in the distance.

"If there are birds," Jared paused and swallowed again. "There is water."

They walked toward the birds. This time, they walked at a quicker pace. Raistlin could barely keep up with the increased gait. The closer the birds were, the more they picked up the pace. Soon they could hear the birds, and when the oasis came into sight, Jared pointed and stood on the tips of his toes like a little boy seeing Mickey Mouse for the first time.

"It's there," Jared said. "I knew it would be."

"Hurry," Dorn said.

Jared broke into a jog, then turned back and put his arm around Raistlin's waist. Dorn and Jared both gained a second wind and dragged Raistlin toward the water.

What was sand and stone under their feet was now grass and wildflowers. The air cooled, and small trees surrounded the body of water that was bigger in size than most ponds. When they reached the water's edge, Jared pulled the fur that draped Raistlin's head and shoulders and tossed it behind him. Then he did the same with his own. Dorn followed suit as they pulled Raistlin into the water.

Jared freed himself from Raistlin and dipped below the surface. He came back up with a satisfied yell. He stood up in the water, which was only halfway up his thighs. He gulped for air, winded from the jaunt.

"Raistlin," Jared smiled. "Take a dip!" Then Jared cupped his hands in the water, held the makeshift bowl to his face, and slurped.

Dorn let go of Raistlin and then submerged into the water.

Jared, reenergized by the refreshing dip, splashed Raistlin. "C'mon, old man!"

Raistlin smiled at the splash, then fell to the side. Jared lurched forward for a second, then stopped as Raistlin floated on his back. Raistlin sprayed water from his mouth straight into the air as he floated. They lounged in the water and drank as much as their stomachs would allow.

As the sun neared evening, Jared asked, "What can we eat around here?"

Raistlin lay in the water with his head on the bank while the rest of his body soaked under the surface. He turned his head and pointed, "That flower over there." His voice was weak and slow, "With the blue edges on it."

Jared looked to where Raistlin was pointing, "Over there?" He pointed. "We can eat those?"

"Yes."

"How do you know this?" Jared asked.

Raistlin looked over at him with a smile, "You've met my daughter, haven't you?"

Jared smiled as he walked toward the shore.

. . .

They ate what plants they could and soaked in the oasis. They had stripped down to their skivvies. Their clothes hung on the trees that surrounded the water. They dreaded what lay before them; they ached at what had happened on the bridge with Billy. Regardless of the relief of the oasis, the reality of events began to sink in.

After a quiet two days of eating, soaking, and hydrating, they donned their dry clothes and headed into the desert under the stars. Although they were limited to the pace that Raistlin could keep, they still made progress.

They hiked for two nights without another sign of water or a set of arches. When the sun began to rise and the heat of the day came with it, Jared spotted something in the distance. A large man-made structure stood; it was too far away to make out exactly what it was. On top of the structure were white specks moving around.

230

"Dorn," Jared said. "Which way is the compass pointing?"

Dorn pulled the compass from his pocket. The needle pointed to the same spot Jared was looking.

"Do you have that telescope thing?" Jared asked.

Dorn pulled the spyglass from another pocket. Jared extended the contraption and held it to his eye. Arches appeared as he looked through the scope. Two levels of opening after opening, all leading to different places. On the top of the structure, two men and two women worked. They swung sledgehammers high into the air and brought them down in an explosion of rock. Jared continued to watch and realized the work crew was slowly destroying the arches. The white specks he saw moving around were hardhats on the workers' heads.

"They're destroying it," Jared said as he handed the spyglass to Dorn.

Dorn looked through the spyglass for a moment. He pulled it down, then put it back up to his eye. "That's our last path to Evergreen," he said. He pulled the spyglass back down, collapsed it, and put it back in his pocket. "That's why they are destroying it, it is their last hope."

"Lance's gods! At it again!" Raistlin said with half-closed eyes while leaning against Dorn.

"We have to go," Dorn said. "If we don't make it, we will be stuck here forever."

"Just think," Raistlin said with a hoarse voice. "We could spend the rest of our days lounging in that pool we were in two days ago."

Dorn pulled Raistlin's arm tighter around his shoulder, "I am not willing to eat those flowers for the rest of my life. Let's go."

For the first time in days, they challenged the heat of the day. It immediately began to take its toll. Before the sun reached its highest point,

Raistlin was on his hands and knees, dry heaving. They kept the furs over their heads to block the sun and kept walking.

They checked the spyglass often as they grew closer to the structure. Rocks and bricks kept tumbling to the base of the arches. Piles began to grow at the entrances of the tunnels.

At one stop, Dorn looked through the spyglass while he gasped for breath. His mouth was open, and his tongue showed a white coating over it. The skin on their fingers and arms sagged and left white imprints when touched. Their tongues stuck to the roofs of their mouths, and talking was nearly impossible.

Once they were able to assess the damage to the structure with their naked eyes, Dorn and Jared began to walk faster as they nearly carried Raistlin along with them. A structure that held almost two dozen arches was now a pile of rubble with only three arches still standing. The four workers looked at them for a moment, then began working at a feverish pace. One red ponytail and one blonde ponytail swung back and forth as the sledgehammer swings of the women quickened.

By the time they reached the base of the rubble, two of the three arches were demolished. They scrambled up the rubble, which was high enough to block half of the opening to the arch. The hammers kept swinging, spraying chips of stone and brick in all directions. They blocked their faces with their furs and clambered over the stones. Once at the top, there was enough room to duck under the arch and into the opening. Dorn went first, then he pulled Raistlin in behind him. Jared followed them as the swings continued from above.

As soon as they disappeared, the entire cave crumbled at once into a pile of rubble. The workers tumbled from their work spots and their hard hats bounced down the mountain of stone. A plume of dust wafted into the air.

Part VII: The Return

Cambria heard the screaming while she was shoeing one of the horses down at the barn. Donte had perked his head and looked toward the hill on the other side of the homestead moments before the screams. Cambria smacked the last tack into the hoof and ran towards the hill. Donte lifted off the ground and flew ahead of Cambria.

"Momma! Nana!" Cambria yelled as she passed the house. The screams continued.

Zelda swooped down before her and Cambria climbed onto the small dragon's back. "Zelda, fly! Follow Donte!"

They flew over the open field and landed in an open area on top of the hill. A young man rolled back and forth on the ground, clutching his leg. He screamed in pain with every breath he had.

Donte, typically very cautious around strangers, looked the man over with his fierce eyes. Then he nudged the man as he lay on the ground like he knew him.

The young man looked up through his curly bangs as Cambria approached. "Cambria," he said and groaned. "Oh, my God! It hurts so bad."

Cambria knelt next to him, "What happened?"

Before he could answer, she said, "Wait, how do you know my name?"

"Cambria," he said. "It's Josh."

She grabbed his shoulders, then pushed his bangs back and looked into his eyes. There was no mistake. Although Jared and Josh never looked alike, Cambria always thought the look of their eyes gave them away as brothers.

"Oh, Great Fathers!" she gasped. "What's happened?"

"It's my leg!" he said through gritted teeth. "I can't stand the pain."

She looked at his leg, which was bare from wearing a pair of shorts. She began to feel around but felt no breaks and didn't see blood.

"Did you sprain something?" she asked.

"Uh, God no. I was hit by a bus or something." He lay on his back and tried to catch his breath. Tears seeped out of the corners of his eyes.

"Oh, no," she whispered. Suddenly, everything began to sink in. Somehow, Josh had been killed in his life on Earth. Tears began to streak down her face.

"My brother was there," Josh said, then grunted as the pain continued. "Jared was with me."

"What?" Cambria said with a confused look on her face.

Josh began to scream again while he clutched his leg and rolled from side to side.

"Can you walk?" Cambria asked him.

Without an answer, he rolled and got to his knees, and then he screamed some more.

Nana and Tessa hurried up the hill and stood by Donte.

"Momma, help me get him on Zelda," Cambria said as she helped Josh to his feet. "Nana, make some chamomile tea and dilute some slumber sand in it; just a pinch."

. . .

Josh's eyes were heavy, and he spoke with a light slur as the tea and slumber sand began to take effect. "Yes, they were all with me," he said and then took a sip of tea. He warmed his hands as he held the cup. "They were fighting in front of an arch. An arch that should have brought them back here."

"Who were they fighting?" Cambria asked.

Josh thought for a moment, then he looked at Cambria. "Lance and Brenna."

She slowly squinted her eyes, "What?"

Josh nodded.

"How did they get there?" Cambria asked as she took a sip of her own tea, this one without slumber sand.

Josh shook his head, "I don't know. But something seems wrong. It seems there are other players in this game." He took another sip of his tea and then looked at her. "Cambria, Raistlin has been there for thirty years." He reached out and held her hand, barely able to keep his eyes open. "He is an old man now."

66

Cambria wiped her eyes as she continued to read from the journal Josh had given her before he zonked out from the medication. Tessa sat motionless on the other side of the dinner table as Cambria read aloud, the smell of coffee wafting out of the cups that sat between them. The rocker Nana sat in squeaked as she rocked and looked out the window.

Cambria closed the journal after she finished the last entry. "So, Daddy is an old man. He, Jared, and Dorn are out there somewhere. Maybe in this Detroit place. Maybe somewhere in Evergreen."

"Maybe In Between."

The three ladies looked up. Josh stood in the bedroom doorway. He limped to the table and sat on the empty seat. He grimaced in pain as he settled into the chair.

Cambria looked at him, waiting for an explanation.

"The In Between," Josh said. "They were fighting near these arches that take you places. I recognized them from when I came here as a kid. It started at home. A small door led to the In Between, then a door or an arch led me to Evergreen." He moved in his seat to try to get comfortable.

Tessa stood, "Josh? Coffee?"

"Yes, ma'am," he said.

"How do you know these were the same kind of arches?" Cambria asked.

"They were," Josh said. "They look the same, or at least they have some kind of aura about them. Once you go through one, you can recognize another one anywhere."

"So, Daddy, Dorn, and Billy could be in this place you are talking about?"

"Or in Detroit, or in Evergreen. Who knows." Josh said. "But Lance was there with us when I got hit and knocked out of my life." He turned his head to the side for a moment and tried to fight a frown. When he regained his composure, he said, "We need to find out if Lance is in Evergreen."

The door of the cabin opened and Sally and Anastasia walked through with the baby in Anastasia's arms.

"Hi!" Anastasia said as she walked toward the table. "We had so much fun staying at Sally's." She stopped when she saw the stranger sitting at the table.

Sally walked up behind Anastasia, looked at the somber group, and said, "What's going on here?"

67

They scrambled around in the dark, calling each other's names. They all coughed from the dust of the collapse.

Jared felt around and found Raistlin, who was half covered in rocks.

"Raistlin," Jared said. "Can you move?"

"Ah," he groaned. "Yes, I can move."

Jared helped him to a sitting position, then said, "Dorn?" It was so dark it was useless to look around to try to find him.

"Right here," Dorn's voice came from Jared's side.

Jared spit out a mouthful of dirt, "Sure could use some water." He spit again and said, "Do we have any flint to try to get a flash of light?"

Without a word, Dorn fumbled around and began to strike the flint. Sparks flew and they tried to get a sense of their surroundings with the quick flashes.

"Just give it up," a voice all too familiar put the striking of the flint to a halt.

The sound of a match being struck was heard, several feet away from them. After the first strike, it was lit. The flame wasn't bright enough to reveal who was behind it. The match went down to the surface and into the glass of an oil lamp. The wick on the lamp came to life. The match was snuffed out, and the wick on the lamp adjusted.

Long dark hair covered the person's face who had lit the lamp. Then the head tilted up, and the hair was pulled from the face.

Lance Erikson sat before them with a smile on his face.

"Well, hello, lads," he said. "Fancy meeting you here in this dirty coal mine."

Layers of black rocks piled behind Dorn, Jared, and Raistlin. The men were covered in dirt. The whites of their eyes were bright in the glow of the flame compared to the darkness of their faces.

"What brings you to these parts?" Lance asked as he looked at them one at a time with a smirk on his face.

"Hmm," he said. "Cat got your tongues?" He scooted a little closer to the lamp, which lit his face more. He looked at Jared and said, "And how did *you* live, war hero?"

"I guess you weren't good enough to kill me," Jared's voice was hoarse with dryness.

Lance laughed, "Oh, I'm good enough. I think you had a little luck on your side, along with a medicine woman." He turned his head and looked at Raistlin, "By the way, old man, I won't be going after Cambria anymore. Her services are no longer needed. My father is dead." He looked from Raistlin to Dorn, "No thanks to you, Dorn. After you chickened out of killing him, he lived several more miserable weeks wasting away and stinking up the top of my castle." Lance squinted his eyes at Dorn, then went on, "But he was a great man. I will miss him."

"He was a murderer," Dorn said through gritted teeth.

Lance leaned back and gasped, "You jest, I am sure."

"He killed my father over a piece of land," Dorn said.

239

"Oh, Mr. Hale. Just because you live in the beautiful world of Evergreen doesn't mean a history of mankind doesn't exist. You don't think that Evergreen might inherit the evils of a world like the one Mr. Collins lived in? Oh, jeepers! Men have killed each other over land for millennia in that world. Hasn't Mr. Barrow read you any history books before you go to bed at night?" He gasped again and put his hand to his mouth, "Speaking of jeepers, did I just do a Billy Blaine?" He turned his head to the side and swept his eyes over the three of them. His earrings reflected in the lamplight. Then he slumped his shoulders and frowned. "What a shame what happened to Billy, falling off the bridge like that because those pesky birds were attacking all of you." He began a sob and dabbed at his eyes with the ends of his black locks. Then he put his finger to his mouth and looked up toward the top of the cave as if he was thinking. "Do you suppose he splatted onto the rocks of the river when he landed? Do you suppose the birds are eating his eyeballs? Oh, wait! They probably already have, they were awfully hungry when I let them loose."

Dorn scrambled to his feet and hissed through his clenched jaw, "I'm going to kill you."

Jared put his arm across Dorn's chest, sending him back to the ground in his weakened state.

Lance began to clap his hands, and he hopped up and down on his butt from his cross-legged position, "Bravo, Mr. Collins. That would be a takedown. So, I score it as Collins, two; Hale, zero." He took in a long breath. "But, really," he said. "The score is Lance infinity, death for the rest of you."

Dorn tried to get to his feet again, but Lance put out his hand. Dorn dropped back to the ground as if a full bushel sack had dropped onto his lap.

"You can't fight me here, Mr. Hale," Lance said. "There is too much magic in my favor. So, fortunately for you, you will never get the chance to lose to me in a fight again. You will die here, along with your other comrades."

"You are a coward," Dorn said quietly, this time not attempting to rise. "Just like your father, you are a coward." He opened his mouth to say more, but his exhaustion held him back.

"Oh, Mr. Hale. There is no reason to be salty about things. It's all water under the bridge, my friend. I forgive you for everything."

"I didn't do anything," Dorn whispered.

Lance smiled, "No, you didn't. Who is the coward now?"

A shot of adrenaline raced through Dorn's veins at the comment. He struggled to his feet; Jared also jumped to his feet. When they stepped toward Lance, he was no longer there. The lamp sat on the floor, along with a cage. Inside the cage sat a small bird, chirping away.

"What?" Jared said. "Where is he?"

"He's gone," Raistlin groaned.

"What's up with the bird?" Jared said.

Dorn shook his head, "I don't know."

"It's a canary," Raistlin said, his voice down to a whisper. "Once the air gets too hard to breathe, the canary will die first. It's a coal mining thing." He leaned forward with great effort. "Lance's gods have the worst in store for us. You must move on." He leaned back and rested against the pile of rocks. "You must go without me. I will only slow you down."

"Raistlin," Jared said.

Raistlin held up his hand, "Listen to me, young man. My daughter needs you."

"Raistlin," Dorn put his hand on Raistlin's shoulder.

Raistlin grabbed Dorn's hand and held it for a moment, then he lifted it to his mouth and kissed it. "It's over, my friend. We will never make it out of here if you drag me along." Raistlin held onto his hand and said, "You'll be fine. Take Jared, go back to Evergreen. Look over my beautiful daughters and watch my grandson grow." He paused for a moment and looked up to the dark ceiling.

"Put a marker at the base of Rickenback Mountain for Billy. He deserves it." He turned his head to the side. "Maybe we will see him in the next world."

68

As bull-headed as Raistlin could be throughout his life, he finally gave in and let the other two lead him through the mine. Raistlin stumbled often, but the others held him up even as weak as they were. Dorn held the lamp in his free hand and Jared held the bird cage in his. The canary's sweet song echoed through the mine, lifting their spirits a bit.

The men were hardly recognizable to each other when the lantern caught their coal-black faces. Their teeth were gritty with dust and dryness.

At times, Raistlin would stop walking, hold his gut, and let out a painful groan. Dorn and Jared would stand and hold him up until he was ready to walk again.

The walk had a gradual drop in elevation. After two stops to rest, they found water. The cave headed upward on the other side of the small pool. Jared released Raistlin's arm and waded in. He held his hands under the water and brought them up in a bowl.

"Dorn," he said. His voice was so hoarse it was barely audible. "The light."

Dorn stepped forward with the lamp held in the air while he still held Raistlin's arm. Jared angled his hands to the light to show black water.

"We can't drink it," he said. Then he slurped a mouthful, swirled it around, and spit it on the floor of the mine. "That feels better," he said. His voice sounded a bit less hoarse. "Raistlin, wash your face off. Just don't swallow any of the water."

After rinsing their faces and swishing the dirty water around their mouths, they moved on. The canary continued to sing brilliant tunes.

Jared stopped walking after they had taken another rest. The others stopped with him. "Dorn, shade the light."

Dorn held the lantern behind his back which shaded the path before them. Jared leaned forward, then said, "I see light, let's keep going."

They moved on, Jared pulling them along with a newfound fervor. At first, the light at the end of the mine was just a small dot in the distance. Then it grew to the size of a BB from a Red Ryder. By the time it was the size of a dime, Jared realized that the canary was no longer singing. He stopped walking and held up the cage, "The bird stopped singing."

Dorn held the lamp in the air. The canary lay on its side at the bottom of the cage.

"It's dead," Jared said.

"That means we are next," Dorn said.

Jared dropped the cage and began walking at a much faster pace. Dorn followed suit, and they dragged Raistlin between them. Soon, Raistlin went completely limp, and his head bobbed forward. Their pace slowed with the lack of momentum.

Jared was the next to succumb to the conditions as he stumbled to the ground. Raistlin fell on top of him, then rolled off to the side. Both men lay limp on the ground. Dorn pulled on Raistlin's clothes and tried to drag him to no avail. Dorn fell to the ground and tried to get up, but only fell back to the ground.

Soon, the three men were unconscious in their own unique, sprawled positions.

69

Donte raised his head and looked back and forth. He and Zelda had just dragged loads of firewood that Hawley, Lawrence, and Zed had cut earlier in the day. The dragons were free for the day, relieved of their duties.

Donte took to the sky, and seconds later, Zelda followed. Hawley walked out of the barn and watched them fly; his hand shielded the sun from his eyes.

Zelda followed Donte as he flew to the top of the hill where it met the base of the stone cliff. He landed with his usual thud, but immediately took a defensive stance when he looked at the stone wall.

The stone wall showed the layers of stratum, the geological layers of sediment that had formed in the rock cliff. But it wasn't the layers of sediment that caught Donte's eye. An arch had formed at the base of the wall. At first, he was cautious, then he began to sniff about the opening.

A familiar scent pulled him to the opening of the cave, but he was too big to enter. He backed out of the opening and raked one of his wings across the ground in frustration.

Zelda came forward and nudged him out of the way. She poked her head into the cave and sniffed for a moment. Then she ducked her head down and walked into the cave. Soon she backed out, dragging a body from her mouth. She set the body on the ground and ventured back into the cave. Donte recognized the body and gave a quick roar; enough of a roar that Hawley would hear it back at the barn.

Zelda removed two more bodies from the cave. By the time Hawley had arrived at the top of the hill, the opening of the cave had disappeared. He looked around as he tried to figure out where the bodies came from; his chest heaved as he caught his breath.

"Is everything okay?" Cambria walked up the hill and Tessa followed, neither of them able to see the three bodies on the ground yet with the dragons and Hawley in the way.

"No," Hawley said and approached the bodies.

Dorn was the first to wake. He propped himself onto his elbows and looked around. He looked as groggy as a man who had taken a twenty year nap.

"Dorn," Cambria said as she approached. "Can you hear me?"

Dorn nodded and scooted to a sitting position.

Jared woke next, and Cambria rushed to his side. She kissed him on the lips and said, "What happened? Why are you so dirty?"

He rolled onto his back, sighed, and said, "Long story."

"Who's…" she began as she looked at the third body, but then stopped when Hawley rolled Raistlin onto his back, revealing his face.

Cambria gasped at the age of her father. His skin was wrinkled, his hair was gray where it wasn't covered with black dust, and he was sunken with hunger and dehydration. She crawled over Jared and put her ear to her father's chest. She listened for a moment, then got to her feet and said, "We have to get him to the cabin. Get Zelda over here."

Hawley led Zelda to Raistlin. Jared and Hawley lifted Raistlin onto Zelda. As Hawley led Zelda down the hill, Cambria turned to Jared and said,

"Your brother is here. So is your son." Then she looked around and asked, "Where's Billy?"

70

After they got Raistlin in the cabin, Dorn and Jared went down to the stream to wash themselves. They came back wearing clean clothes that Tessa had delivered to the stream bank.

"How is he?" Dorn asked Cambria when they were back in the cabin. Cambria's eyes were swollen from crying.

"Weak," Cambria said and looked toward the doorway of the bedroom where Raistlin lay in a bed, slipping in and out of consciousness. "I can't believe how old he looks." She looked back at Dorn and asked, "Why was he there so long?"

Dorn shook his head, "The Great Fathers messed up."

"How?" Cambria asked.

"I don't know," Dorn said. "But, I plan to find out."

"Where's Billy?" Anastasia stood in the doorway of the cabin with a basket of berries held at her side. Dorn turned to her, and the look on his face told the story. She dropped the basket and ran out the door.

Cambria wiped her eyes.

71

Jared's return to Evergreen was a whirlwind. Time between his old world and Evergreen was fickle; the aging of Raistlin while he was gone for only a short period of time was a testament to that. While he was in Detroit, it never crossed his mind that Cambria would have the baby while he was gone. He also found out that Josh was in Evergreen, which only meant that in his old world, Josh was gone. Jared's parents had lost both of their sons. That filled Jared with an overwhelming amount of sadness. The fact that Raistlin was dying and Billy was gone, forever this time, added salt to the wound.

Earlier, on their way back to the cabin from the bath in the stream, Cambria had walked out of the cabin and down the porch steps with the baby in her arms. Jared broke down when he held his son. Tears rolled off his face onto the baby's head.

"I named him Sawyer," Cambria wiped at one of Jared's tears. "Just like we had agreed if it was a boy."

When Jared regained his composure, Dorn put his arm around him and said, "How wonderful, to have another baby in Evergreen. I hope Raistlin wakes soon to see this."

Soon, Jared was at his brother's side. Josh slept from the effects of another pain remedy concocted by Cambria. Jared sat and stared at his brother and wondered about their parents. A motion through the window caught his eye. He lowered his head to see what it was. A horse and rider trotted up the dirt road leading to the homestead. The horse slowed, and Sally slid off the saddle. She ran a few steps, then Dorn came into view. She leaped to him when he was close enough, and he caught her and spun her around. They engaged in a long kiss, then he put her down so she was on her feet again. Dorn placed his hands on Sally's shoulders and spoke. Sally brought her hands to her mouth and her eyes opened wider. Jared could almost hear her gasp from inside the cabin. She began to fall to her knees, but Dorn caught her. She leaned into him and sobbed.

Cambria brought Jared a bowl of soup and two biscuits. He ate as he watched his brother sleep. When he was sopping the last of the broth in the bowl with his remaining biscuit, Josh woke.

"Hey, kid," Jared said with half of a biscuit in his hand.

"Jare," Josh whispered and looked around. "You're back."

"And so are you," Jared said.

"Does this mean I'm dead?" Josh said, then winced as he swung his legs over the side of the bed.

"I think it means we may be stuck here in Evergreen for good," Jared said.

"Mom and Dad," Josh whispered as he gazed at the floor.

"I know," Jared said. He paused for a moment, then said, "Josh."

Josh lifted his gaze from the floor and met his brother's eyes.

"Billy's gone," Jared said in a cracked voice.

Josh sucked in a small gasp, "What?"

"He's gone. We lost him in the In Between."

"How? He was with us in Detroit," Josh paused for a moment, then spoke a little quieter, "In Detroit, when my life got ripped away."

251

"Remember that big bird-looking thing that cut my shoulders in the Dark Forest?"

Josh squinted his eyes and gave a small nod.

"We were crossing this rope bridge when they started attacking us. Billy got knocked over and couldn't hang on." Jared stopped for a moment and looked out the window. "We couldn't get to him. We're probably lucky Raistlin didn't fall off the bridge as well."

"How is he?" Josh asked as he winced again. "How's Raistlin?"

"It's pretty bad. It took us a long time to get here."

72

"He left this for you," Sally handed Dorn a folded up letter, then took a sip of her whiskey. They sat at a table in the corner of the saloon. Dorn opened it and tilted it toward a window to read it better.

Mr. Hale,

I'd rather not give my name in a letter, but I am a lifelong resident of Greystone.

I am a worker at Erikson's Castle and could be of assistance to you and Mr. Barrow.

I can give you more details if we meet in person. I will arrive at the base of the bridge crossing the Snake River every fifth day at sunset. Whenever someone is ready to meet, have them cross the bridge. When they see me step onto my end of the bridge, they shall turn back to Ironwood. Then I will know to follow.

There are things happening here that need to stop.

Please, let's meet so we can talk.

Your friend,
The stranger from Greystone

"How did he seem?" Dorn asked as he read the letter over again.

"He seemed genuine," Sally said as Dorn began to fold the letter. "Like a man with passion. I think it's worth meeting with him."

"When will he be back at the bridge?" Dorn asked as he stuffed the letter into the inside of his leather vest.

"Tomorrow at sunset."

"I'll make sure I am here."

. . .

Dorn saw the man on the other end of the bridge as the sun touched the horizon behind him. He nudged Cherokee with his heels and led him up the approach of the bridge. Then Dorn led the horse to a trot. Once they reached mid-span of the bridge, he spun the horse and raced back, leaving a cloud of dust behind.

A short time later, Jenn pointed toward Dorn sitting in the corner as a man approached the bar with a question. The man looked; Dorn, sitting with his hand around his glass that sat on the table, lifted a finger and gave a quick nod in acknowledgment.

The man sat down across from Dorn. His wide-brim hat was low on his forehead, but once he was comfortable in his chair, he pulled the hat from his head and set it on the chair beside him.

"Hello," the man said in a nervous voice.

Dorn nodded and asked, "What are you drinking?"

The man had long hair with a beard to match and tattoos on his arms. He nodded at Dorn's glass and said, "I'll take one of those."

Dorn looked to Jenn and held up two fingers. He looked back at the man and said, "What is it you wish to talk about?"

"I saw you and Raistlin fight Lance at the foot of the castle several moons ago," the man said.

Dorn nodded slowly.

"I'm sorry about your friend that was killed there," the man said.

Dorn glanced down at the table and frowned for a moment, "Me too."

"Bad things have been happening in Greystone," the man fidgeted with his fingernails for a moment, then he looked up at Dorn. "Bad things. For a long time."

"I am not surprised."

"We need help," the man leaned forward, then sat back while Jenn set two glasses of whiskey on the table. The man slouched back and he took a sip of the brown liquid.

Dorn waited for the man to continue.

The man leaned forward again and said, "My name is Teagan. I'd stand like a gentleman and shake your hand, but I shouldn't even be here."

"I understand," Dorn said.

"I have a plan," Teagan said. "And a partner."

"Who is your partner?"

Teagan took another sip and said, "Someone very dear to me. Someone that I trust." His hand went to his beard for a moment, then fell back on his lap. "We could run from Greystone." His eyes drifted to the side then he said, "But we have to do something. Too many things are happening."

They finished their whiskeys and agreed to meet at the base of the bridge in five days.

73

Dorn waited at the bank of the river behind a copse of trees. He looked up toward the opposite side of the bridge and could picture the winding road that led to the bridge, but was unable to see it from where he stood. Dorn held no intentions of meeting Teagan this time. He knew Teagan's pleas were genuine, but he wanted to be sure of his honesty and dedication. The man was playing a dangerous game.

Dorn had others watching as Teagan made his way down the road that led through the woods. Two men were hiding halfway between the bridge and Greystone, and Teddy Thorton was stationed behind his barn. The request was an easy one for Teddy; all he had to do was fish on his own property, keep an eye out for anything out of the ordinary, and determine if Teagan was alone. Dorn loaned him his spyglass so Teddy could get a better look when the time came. Once nightfall hit, he would report to Emily, who would take the info back to Dorn.

Dorn saw Teagan approach the bridge on foot. Teagan stopped at the base of the crossing and waited. He didn't appear to be nervous or fidgety, and he leaned against a post on the side of the road. A short time later, nightfall engulfed the area. Teagan turned and headed back to Greystone, the moon lighting his way down the stone road.

Dorn made his way up the riverbank and walked into town and to the saloon. Sally came out of the back of the saloon and joined him at the bar. He slipped a coin across the walnut topped surface when two whiskeys appeared. Since Sally had been elected mayor, Dorn never ran up a tab at the bar, and he always made sure he paid for Sally's drinks, too. He considered Sally and himself as typical townspeople, no different than anyone else. There would be no special privileges for the husband of the mayor.

After a few short conversations and a drink with Emily, Dorn learned that Teagan had traveled alone with his head tucked under his hat and his collar flipped up on his coat when he left Greystone. There was no sign of funny business whatsoever.

Dorn, satisfied with the results, decided he would meet the man in five more days.

74

Dorn led Cherokee down the dusty road on the way to Rickenback Mountain. Cherokee pulled a wagon with Nana and Tessa in the seat. Behind them, America pulled a wagon with Sally and Anastasia. Josh lay on blankets in the back and grimaced in pain when the wagon took the occasional bump in the road. Cambria walked down the road next to Jared as he led America with the reins. Sawyer was sleeping in the leather contraption that hung from Cambria's neck and shoulders.

Raistlin lay in bed in a stupor back at the cabin, too weak to attend the funeral of Billy Blaine.

Dorn stopped Cherokee at a spot they had chosen, and he reached up and helped Nana and Tessa down from the seat of the wagon. All of them but Dorn and Jared made their way to a clearing in the grass. In the middle of the clearing, the short grass had been pulled away.

Dorn and Jared reached into the back of one of the wagons and slid a rock to the edge. Then they slid the rock off the end of the wagon and carried it to the clearing. Their feet moved quickly as they struggled with the heavy object. They placed the rock on the back side of the torn away grass. The face of the rock read "Billy Blaine," chiseled in the smooth surface by Dorn with the help of the local blacksmith.

Most of the stone markers at the base of Rickenback Mountain had bodies buried in the dirt below them. There were a few that did not. Those few were ones that went on expeditions and never returned. Their lives were still remembered at the foot of the mountain. Billy Blaine was about to join that elite group.

They gathered in a semicircle, all of them facing the stone. In typical circumstances, Raistlin led ceremonies like this. They all waited for Dorn to step forward.

After a moment, he did. He pulled something from his pocket. He took a deep breath and looked up at the sky for a moment. Then his gaze fell down to Billy's stone, and he spoke, "I met Billy Blaine in the middle of the night under the light of the moons. Together we flew on the back of Celeste and made it here." Dorn paused for a moment and wiped a tear from his eye. Some of the others began to sob. "Billy immediately became a part of my life," he spread out his hands and continued. "A part of my family." He stepped forward and said, "I'll never forget you, Billy." He set a coin onto the bare ground in front of the stone. Billy had given him the coin when they were together in Detroit.

"Dorn," Billy had said as he held the quarter to him. "This one was made the year I met Josh."

Dorn had taken the coin, and on the bottom, it read, "1962." He smiled at Billy and handed it back.

"No, it's yours," Billy smiled. "A gift."

The coin sparkled in the sunlight as it lay on the dirt.

Anastasia walked forward and unhooked the clasp of a necklace she wore.

One morning before Jared and Dorn had returned with Raistlin, Anastasia woke with a necklace and a small amethyst pendant around her neck. For a moment, she had a flashback of her life on Earth, something that had never happened to her before. Billy always told her she had a life on Earth, but she remembered none of it until that moment. Billy had gifted the necklace to her on a special occasion that she couldn't recall. She sat up in bed and looked down at the necklace as she remembered the moment. Then dread swarmed over her as she realized something must be terribly wrong. Days later she learned that Billy was gone.

Josh had an odd experience as well. When he was thrust out of his life on Earth, he wound up in Evergreen. After he had settled in the cabin and was comfortable, he noticed something in the back pocket of his jeans. He reached back and pulled out an old, beat up Detroit Tigers baseball cap. The cap had pinstripes on the front with a tiger as a logo. Josh had never seen one quite like it, and knew it was something from Billy's life. He, too, was overwhelmed with sadness.

Anastasia walked forward, stooped down, and laid the necklace on the bare ground. She stepped back and said, "I love you, Billy Blaine." Tears streamed down her cheeks.

Josh walked forward and set the cap on the ground next to the coin and the necklace.

Jared and Dorn walked forward and lifted the rock to the bare spot, covering the relics that were left behind.

Josh fell to his knees and began to sob. The loss of Billy, his exit from his previous life, the thought of his parents suffering such huge losses, and Samira. It all came crashing down at once. He leaned forward and put his forehead on the ground as he cried.

Jared walked to him, stooped down, and put his arms around Josh as the others tried not to watch. All of them wept.

75

A few days after the funeral, Dorn trotted Cherokee to the halfway point of the bridge. He saw Teagan waiting on the other side. When he turned his horse and trotted back, Teagan took the bridge by foot and quickly followed.

Dorn sat at the usual table in the corner of the saloon. Teagan approached and sat, once again setting his hat on the chair next to him.

"I have news," Teagan said.

Dorn held his finger up for a moment as Jenn approached with two drinks. She set them on the table and walked off.

"Go on," Dorn said as he slid one of the whiskeys in front of Teagan.

Teagan looked around for a moment, then leaned toward Dorn. "I have found Billy Blaine," he whispered.

Dorn almost had the small glass to his lips, but he stopped when he heard Teagan's words. "What?"

"Billy Blaine, your friend," Teagan whispered even quieter than before. "I have found him."

Dorn set the glass on the table and glared at Teagan, "Is he alive?"

Teagan nodded. "Yes," he said. "He is alive and well."

Thank you for reading *The Stories of Evergreen Book II: Pawns of the Inbetween*. If you haven't read where the story started, pick up a copy of *The Stories of Evergreen Book I: The Life of Billy Blaine*.

Find out more at www.rshamilton.com.

VC

www.ingramcontent.com/pod-product-compliance
Lightning Source LLC
Chambersburg PA
CBHW022034240626
47154CB00007B/2394